LORD SEBASTIAN AND THE SCOTTISH LASS

A Seabrook Family Saga, Book Four

CHRISTINE DONOVAN

Sign up for Christine's newsletter to be informed of new releases and to be eligible for special contests and prizes. You can sign up on Christine's website at http://www.christinedonovan.org/

❀ Created with Vellum

This book is dedicated to the members of RIRW (Rhode Island Romance Writers). Without you, your support and encouragement over the years, none of this would be possible.

The very first time I walked into a meeting, I looked around the room at all the welcoming smiles and I knew I found the group I would belong to forever.

I love you all!

I want to thank my husband, Michael and my four sons, Shawn, Matt, Danny and Joey for all your support and understanding over the years when dinner was late and the laundry didn't get done. My mother, Alberta Murray, and my sister, Karen Gomer, for always being there for me and listening to me share my ideas for new stories. Joanne Smart for being my first reader and always being honest and having great feedback.

Chapter One

NORTHERN ENGLAND

JAGGED BOLTS OF LIGHTNING FOLLOWED BY EAR SPLITTING thunder caused every muscle in Sebastian Seabrook's body to constrict. Halfpenny sized raindrops pelted him from every conceivable direction as the wind howled relentlessly. His tired and frightened gelding needed shelter, as did he. *Why on earth did I volunteer to go on this mission?*

When next the lightning bolt lit up the scarcely traveled muddy road, it struck a tree in close proximity. The explosion shook the ground beneath him. His horse, spooked, reared up nearly unseating him and then bolted. Not down the muddy road, but into the woods. Sebastian fought with the reins, gave up the struggle to keep them in his hands and leaned far forward wrapping his arms around his horse's neck and holding on for his life. "Please God," he prayed. "I only wish to go home."

Each and every time the sky lit up, he realized his horse carried them deeper and deeper into the unknown forest. If Sebastian had not been lost before, he certainly was now. His brother, the Duke, had wanted to hire Bow Street Runners for this quest, but no, he'd volunteered against his family's wishes. He could hear the conversation clear as day inside his head even now over the noise of the storm raging around him.

"I will go," Sebastian Seabrook, *the younger brother to the Duke of Wentworth said to his family as they discussed what to do about a mysterious missive they received from a young girl claiming to be their father's natural born daughter.*

"You want to go?" questioned Wentworth.

"Why not?" Sebastian sipped his tea and took a mouthful of biscuit. "I have nothing keeping me here and the official Season has ended. Why you insist on the family staying in London in the heat of the summer is beyond me."

"Yes, well." Wentworth cleared his throat. "Since my lovely wife, Emma, is expecting, I believe we will retire to the country for several months. Why don't you join us and leave this investigation to our friend, Mr. Smythe."

"Because I have to go."

Didn't his family understand? He needed to get away and clear his head. Find purpose in his life. Ever since the one person he thought he would wed left him, he'd drifted in a sea of uncertainty. He needed to find himself again and perhaps this quest would help him. Also, he wanted to bring the girl home to his family safe and sound.

Marissa Frederickson, the woman he thought he would marry—eventually—fell in love with a military man and to her brother's shock ran off. Bloody hell, she just left without a word to Sebastian or anyone else for that matter. He couldn't honestly say his heart was broken, but it pained nonetheless. He and Marissa had been friends since childhood, and everyone thought they would marry in due time. How had they all been wrong, including him?

Now Sebastian had no prospects. Nor did the thought of spending time in the country appeal to him. The thought of traveling to Northern England seeking his dead father's natural daughter seemed as good an idea as any to break free from the monotony of London in the off Season.

Lightning struck close again and he yelled, "Bloody hell, will this storm never abate." His horse began to tire, but he didn't slow. More spooked than ever he continued on. The rain intensified, which Sebastian didn't think was possible, but it did. He didn't risk letting one hand free from gripping his horse's mane to wipe the cold rainwater from his eyes, therefore, he could barely make out his horse's ears, never mind where they were headed.

Suddenly, his horse stopped, spun around and reared up, this time unseating Sebastian. The ground crashed up to meet him with such force it stole his breath away. Then just as quickly, the soaking ground vanished and he went sliding down. Mud, rocks, tree branches tore painfully into his body. He threw his arms up protecting his head. He tumbled still, hit something hard, rock or tree, it didn't matter as pain exploded throughout his thigh and arm. At least he stopped falling.

Having come to rest on his back, he took quick breaths to fight the nauseating pain and the spinning of his head. Sebastian tried to lean up and look at his now numbing leg but couldn't manage it and groaned as he lay back. Every part of his body screamed in agony, and he didn't have the energy or will to move. All he wanted to do was close his eyes and rest, but he knew it would be the death of him. So he fought it to no avail. The sound of the rain hitting the trees and leaves and splashing onto the mud soaked ground soothed him and he slept to escape the pain, the cold, and the drenching rain.

"Wakey, wakey, govner."

The first thing Sebastian became aware of was a man's voice and a boot shoving relentlessly into his aching side. The second thing he became aware of was every part of his body hurt like bloody hell.

Where was he?

What had happened?

Then he remembered the storm, his horse bolting and throwing him, then falling down some kind of embankment. He didn't want to open his eyes. He didn't want to wake up. Being awake meant pain, unbearable, unforgiving agonizing pain.

"Wake up." Another set of boots came into his field of vision.

This time the boot stomped on his stomach. Sebastian curled partway on his side and retched up what little food he'd consumed that day.

"For the love of God, leave me be," he croaked as he squinted, trying to make out the men belonging to the voices and the confounded boot.

"Oh, dinnae you worry, govner," one of the men drawled. "Once we have what we want, we'll leave you." Sick laughter surrounded him. "Of course once we leave, you'll be meeting your maker."

Sebastian struggled to rise, to no avail. His body was wounded more than he realized. "I'll pay you. Just leave me be."

Strong hands patted him down, tearing his cloak and boots from his battered body. Then he heard the unmistakable sound of his coin purse being tossed around. "Seems we found ourselves a rich noble."

Sebastian reached out with his good arm. "There is more where that came from. My family will pay greatly for my safe return."

"We are nay do-gooders."

Sebastian watched with horror as one of the men raised his foot and crashed it down on his head. Pain exploded, and right before darkness descended, his body was kicked and he began to tumble once again. Only this time when he stopped, freezing water splashed around him.

"Hurry Lachlan," they are getting away."

"What would ye have me do, sister of mine, give chase tae the highwaymen or save the poor mon's life?"

Lady Teagan Murray put her hands on her hips and glared at her twin. "Weel, by the looks of him, he is already dead."

Her brother knelt by the man, put his hand on his chest, his ear near his mouth. "He lives. Hurry, help me drag him out of the water."

Teagan sighed, marched over and grabbed the man's bootless feet while her brother took the arms. Stepping into the ankle deep water didn't matter to her as her boots and clothing were already soaking wet thanks to the torrential rain. As they tugged the body, an inhuman sound fell from the man's lips, then silence.

"Ah believe he came tae only tae pass out again," Lachlan said. "No wonder he yelled. Look at his arm and leg. We need tae see tae his injuries immediately. Hand me something tae stop his leg from bleeding. 'Tis sliced right tae the bone and bleeding like a sieve."

Teagan used her teeth to tear a strip of cloth off her borrowed shirt and tied it high up the stranger's thigh, hoping to squelch the bleeding. If it didn't work he would be dead within minutes.

"Do ye think 'tis wise tae bring him home?" Teagan winced at the bloody, raw gash that ran from the stranger's temple to his jaw. "Paw could have sent him? You ken he has loyal mon scouring all of Scotland and England looking for us?"

"Even if he's one of Paw's mon, he willnae be going

anywhere anytime soon." His eyes went from the man to their horses. "Besides, he's dressed tae fine. A Sassenach ah believe. Where is yer compassion?"

Teagan huffed. "Since we're hiding for our lives, having compassion for a stranger could prove dangerous."

"I'm hiding for my life," Lachlan reminded her. "Ye lassie are hiding from the monster our paw betrothed ye tae."

Teagan waved her arm out. "If Paw gets his hands on us, we are both dead and ye verra weel know it."

"Come lass, help me get him over the back of my horse."

"Have ye taken a good look at him? He is massive." Her brother may be equal in size to the stranger, but she was petite and according to her father, scrawny to boot.

"Just take his bloody feet and let's get going before he dies."

It took all her and Lachlan's strength to swing the man up and over on his belly on the backside of the horse. Once again wounded animal sounds came from his lips that sent chills up her spine. Her brother wanted to know where her compassion was. It burst alive inside her chest when she got a closer look at the man's bruised and battered body and face. Her mother, God rest her soul, had taught her how to nurse the sick, bandage wounds, and set bones. But even she didn't think she could save this man's life.

They traveled to the outskirts of a small village, near Northumberland, to a neat two-room dwelling where they hurried to get the man inside before anyone witnessed. They dropped him as gently as they could on her bed in the one small bedchamber. "Ye undress him, while ah get water heated and clean linen," Teagan said as she grabbed a pail and went outside to the well to draw fresh water. While the water heated in a kettle on the fire, she rummaged through her clothing and paused briefly before she tore her last un-tattered chemise into strips.

"Teagan, ah need help here, and bring a sharp knife," Lachlan bellowed.

"Coming," she replied as she grabbed a knife, the cloth and water with her.

"I'll hold him still while ye cut away his clothing."

Taking a deep breath, she ignored the man's face, twisted up in agony, and cut away first his waistcoat, shirt, then cravat. She breathed deeply at her first sight of his well-muscled chest sprinkled with blond hair that trailed down in a line into his trousers. Swallowing the sudden lump in her throat, she grabbed those muddy, wet trousers and carefully cut down both sides, aware that one slip of the knife and she could end his plans to have a family.

"Careful," Lachlan breathed.

"Ah am...perhaps we should cover him before..."

"Don't turn all girly on me now, lass. You took care of Uncle Colin during his last days."

"Aye, but he was old. Oh my." Her hands flew to her cheeks, which burned to her touch.

Lachlan grabbed a sheet and covered the lower half of their guest, sparing her virgin eyes, but not before she got an eyeful. He picked up the knife she had dropped onto the bed and finished removing the man's clothing. "Let's repair the mon's leg first. I'll hold his body while ye do it."

Teagan inspected the man's thigh and sighed with relief that it was not broken. She set to work with needle and thread she'd sterilized with brandy. It was all the harder to concentrate because the sheet kept moving dangerously close to exposing his manhood again. As she struggled to sew the enormous gash, the man screamed louder than she'd ever heard and he fought Lachlan, only to pass out again which was a blessing. "Ah need something to keep it stable otherwise the stitching is going to be terrible and the mon's scar horrendous tae look at."

"Set the arm now while he's unconscious, then go back tae the leg."

Setting the arm proved uneventful. While her brother hunted for a splint, she went back to her sewing. Several times she paused to stretch her sore body. Helping to carry the heavy man had strained her lower back. Finally she tied off the last stitch and removed the tourniquet to get the blood flowing through his leg again before it did any permanent damage. She dipped clean linen into warm water and bathed the blood from his leg. Then she needed to inspect the rest of his body for more wounds. She wiped the dirt from his face. The cut down his cheek would need stitching as well. Gently, she roamed her fingers through his thick sandy hair and came upon a deep gash. As she cleaned it, he moaned and opened one eye wide. She gasped at the pain and confusion she glimpsed in that startling blue orb.

He licked his lips and whispered, "Who are you?"

"Dinnae move. Ye are hurt. My brother and ah will care for ye."

"How..."

Before he could mutter another word his eyes rolled back in his head, and he passed out again. She ran her fingertips over his skull once more, looking for signs of a fracture. She believed he had a small one. That would explain why he kept passing out. Actually, if he stayed unconscious for a day or two it might be better for his healing. Of course, if he turned out to be one of Father's men, she hoped he never gained consciousness. But until the truth came known, she would help and heal him. It wasn't in her nature to be unkind.

After washing the rest of his body, excluding the part between his large solid thighs, she poured some brandy on the cuts, causing him to wince in his sleep. Cleaning needle and thread once again she set to work stitching his face. Even with the gash and one swollen eye, she admitted he was handsome. More handsome than most of the men she knew. And compared to the brut her father wanted her to marry, this man's looks were angelic and her so-called betrothed the devil. But still she felt uneasy over his presence. Could he be trusted with their secrets?

The laceration on his face was deep, down to the cheekbone. She believed it best to set a row of stitches inside then another row of tiny ones pulling the skin together much like she'd done with his thigh. Teagan took painstaking care to make small numerous stitches on the surface to keep the scar minimal. No need to mark his handsome face with a grotesque scar.

Lachlan came back with two pieces of small wood and he wrapped the man's arm, keeping it stable so the bones could knit together straight. All she could do was pray his arm wouldn't be damaged, his thigh would heal, and he would walk again. She did her best to set the bone and stitch him up, the rest was up to God.

Teagan hurried to the main room, took a jar off the shelf, and went back to their patient. After washing her hands she used her fingers to gently coat all his cuts with her homemade remedy. It would keep infection away and aid in the healing.

"Ye did well lass," Lachlan said as his fingers worked fast to tie the last knot of cloth on the man's arm. "Has he woken at all?"

"Once. He said 'how' then his blue eyes rolled back into his head. Which reminds me ah need to wrap a cloth around his head. He has a deep abrasion on the back and ah felt a slight fracture."

"How is it ye noticed his eye color when ye were busy attending to his wounds?" Lachlan gave her his signature crooked grin and one brow raised look. A look many young lasses back in Scotland would willingly give their innocence to see.

Heat tinged her cheeks. "Hard tae miss when one intense eye was concentrated on me." Thinking about that one good eye clouded with pain and confusion made her want to help him recover so she could see them both, clear and pain free. She shivered at the thought of having his eyes riveted on hers.

"Why has yer face turned red?"

She tossed a cloth at Lachlan. "It isnae." She frowned as she studied the man's face. "Who do ye think he is? Can we trust him even though I suspect he is English? He could still be working for Paw? All that aside, is his family or perhaps a wife frantic with worry wondering where he is? Is he alive? I didnae see a third horse with the highwaymen, where do ye suppose his mount went off too?" Gently she wrapped a clean bandage around his head. It took all her will to concentrate on the task at hand and not get lost in his almost boyish good looks. Why did sleeping men always resemble innocent young boys when all their features were relaxed in rest? Even evil men could look innocent in sleep. Was this stranger, perhaps an enemy? Although she didn't think so. After finishing tying the bandages, she moved an errant lock of hair out from his eyes. Eyes she could hardly wait to see again.

What was she thinking? Recently she managed to escape the clutches of the meanest, cruelest man in all of Scotland, she didn't need to be thinking of this one.

"Will ye stay with him whilst ah heat up the stew leftover from yesterday?"

AFTER HIS SISTER LEFT, Lachlan studied the unconscious man and wondered what spell he cast on Teagan. He'd never seen her take such care with a patient, or blush profusely, never mind the longing look in her eyes as she tended him. As much as his instincts made him believe the man wasn't one of his father's henchmen, he had an uneasy tingle in his spine. They had to keep their true identity from this man. They would have to abstain from using their given names while in his company.

Rising from the old battered wooden chair with the wobbly legs, he went into the main room and stood by his sister's side as she heated the stew in the large fireplace. "We need tae use the names we adopted when we escaped from Murray Castle, Maggie and Brice McHugh. And remember our story about our parents' dying two months ago and we sought relatives here in Northumberland only tae find they had moved on. So we decided tae stay and find work."

"Do ye really think 'tis necessary with this mon?"

More of those infernal tingles traveled up and down his spine. "Aye, ah bloody hell do.

TWO MONTHS EARLIER

Murray Castle
Scotland

WITNESSING HER MOTHER TAKE HER LAST BREATH AND GO to the afterlife, Teagan hugged herself and shivered with uncertainty. Her mother was all that stood between her and her father. Who would keep him from insisting she marry that barbarian, Malcolm MacPherson? It was 1818 and the man still lived like it was medieval times. Tears rolled down her face as much for her mother as for herself and her fragile future. Her mother had suffered greatly the past months and Teagan sighed with relief, knowing she was in a far better place now, but couldn't she have lived a little bit longer? Kept her and her twin brother safe for a while longer?

If her father had his way he would send her off to MacPherson and see the wedding take place this evening. Why was it so important to him that she marry that man? The clans were not at war, so why? Was the man's loyalty to her father that necessary? Did her father have greedy plans in the workings? Not having these answers had her wanting to scream at the top of her lungs. It wasn't herself alone she worried about. Their father hated her brother, Lachlan. Teagan had no idea when the hatred began, or for what reason. All she could remember was it was always so. Father loved his youngest son, Ian. With their mother gone to keep the peace, what would happen to them?

She had not long to find out. On the eve of her mother's burial, as she readied herself for bed with a heavy heart, someone knocked on her door. Believing it to be Lachlan, she opened it without asking and was thrown back when MacPherson, the man she feared most besides her father, stormed through the door. Slamming it closed, he turned the key she always left in the lock, pocketed it, and leered at her with lust filled black eyes.

"What is the meaning of this?" Teagan questioned with bravado that didn't exist as she backed up, her eyes wide. Fear unlike any she'd ever known gripped her insides.

"Yer paw has given me ye. We will marry in the morning." His beady eyes roamed up and down her body making her skin crawl.

"Then our wedding night will take place tomorrow." Try as she might to appear calm and in control her voice trembled as she said the words. "Not this evening."

Roaring laughter shook the giant of a man dressed in a filthy tartan. The dirt was so thick it coated the fabric and his body to the extent she could not make out the pattern of his clan. Obviously he didn't believe in bathing on a regular basis —or ever. "According to yer paw, ye belong tae me now, and ah can do as ah want." He stepped closer to her, his putrid breath nearly felling her as he reached out his grimy hand to squeeze her breast painfully. She batted his hand away and rage flashed in his eyes, quickly to be replaced with lust again.

He chuckled. "Ye like it rough? Ye want tae spank me and I'll spank ye?"

As he lunged for her and rolled on top of her, she clawed at his face, drawing blood. It didn't deter him. The sound of cloth ripping vibrated in her ears and cool air landed on her exposed skin. In a matter of seconds he'd rendered her naked. *Oh my God, I would rather die than submit tae this animal. How could Paw do this tae me?*

Maybe she could stall for time by engaging him in conversation. "Malcolm, please tell me about yerself and yer clan? I ken nothing about ye and wish tae get tae ken ye better."

"Stop squawking lass. I like my women either moaning or screaming. A woman's mouth should be used for eating food or for sucking cock. Get used tae my rules now and we'll get along just fine."

He could not be serious. Suck...his...Tears pooled in her eyes, and she was afraid she might be sick at the thought of putting her mouth anywhere on this disgusting creature.

Every muscle in her body tensed when his knee forcefully parted her legs and he rose up, lifted his tartan, giving her an eyeful of his grotesquely engorged sex. "Nay, nay, nay," she moaned as she closed her eyes and willed her brain to tell her what to do. She would not let that...that thing soil her body. Then she remembered something Lachlan told her. "If a mon forces himself on ye, hurt him between his legs. Either knee him or grab him with yer hands and twist and squeeze with all yer strength."

But how? Her legs were pinned beneath his lower body eliminating the knee. She uncurled her hand, reached down and filled her palm with his large hairy balls and with every ounce of energy she yanked and twisted.

An animalistic scream burst from his lips, he cupped himself, fell on top of her and vomited onto the floor, barely missing her head. Using her arms she shoved him off her then scrambled to her feet seeking escape. The only way out was the locked heavy wooden door or the window three stories up. She would take her chances and throw herself out the window if necessary. Death would be welcome.

She knew her time was running out as MacPherson struggled to stand. "Ah will kill ye bitch." He growled.

Without thinking about her choices, she threw the dress she'd worn that day on, grabbed her boots and headed to the window, but she paused at the sound of someone banging on her door.

"Teagan, Teagan, are ye in there?" Lachlan yelled.

"Lachlan, help me. Malcolm's in here. He tried tae rape me."

"Open the door."

"He has the key."

Her enemy was on his feet coming toward her, murder in his eyes. She was forced toward the fireplace. Reaching out blindly, she grabbed the wrought iron poker and swung at his head with all her might. He went down and landed in a twisted heap. His head oozed copious amounts of blood, and she fought the bile rising up her throat. She put her trembling fingers in his filthy sporran and removed her room key. She ran to the door, fingers shaking so badly it took her three tries to get the key in the lock and turn it to let her brother in. Lachlan stepped inside and quickly locked the door behind him.

"Quick, pack a satchel, we leave now." Lachlan, gripping his drooping shoulder, went to MacPherson and inspected him. "Damn, he still lives."

"What happened to ye?" Her eyes widened in shock to see the blood soaking through his white shirt.

"Paw shot me. He wants me dead. We must leave now."

"Not until ah tend yer wound." As she spoke she hurried to her healing herbs on her dressing table.

"Nay. Do ye want that thing tae awaken and finish what he started with ye?"

"God nay."

Afraid to light a candle, they used their hands to feel their way through the pitch dark castle. Teagan's heart pounded so loud in her chest, she thought her father would hear it wherever he was. When they reached the servants staircase, she wanted to breathe a sigh of relief but knew it was too soon to believe they were safe. Their servants might dislike her father, but they were terrified of him and would betray her and Lachlan to save from being beaten or worse. Lachlan paused at the door to the outside.

"Taking horses is tae risky, we go on foot," he whispered.

As her brother slowly opened the thankfully well-oiled heavy door, the crisp night breeze caressed her face. They took a moment to adjust their sight to the darkness. Clouds prevented the moon from lighting up an escape path for them. However, under the midnight dark sky, they could sneak away without being spotted by their father's men.

They hurried across the expanse of green lawn. Teagan barely breathed as they ran. She expected to hear shouts from her father's men giving them away. When silence stayed with them, they pushed on into the cover of the forest.

"Ah realize 'tis dangerous tae keep going in the dark, but we must. We need tae put as many miles between us and Paw," Lachlan said breathlessly. "Because when he finds us gone, he will send his most experienced soldiers and trackers after us."

"Aye. Ah agree."

"Stay close on my heels. I'll try tae keep ye safe from low lying branches. We are not taking the path. They will come on horseback and be upon us quickly."

"How long will it take us tae travel on foot tae Grandpaw's or our uncles?"

"We go tae England."

Because of the darkness she could not see Lachlan's face, but by the sadness in his voice she shivered and not from the chilly night air. Afraid to ask, but knowing she had to she said, "Why?"

"Because Paw had them killed."

"Killed?" she cried out, then covered her mouth with her hand. They needed to be silent or they would be dead as well. Tears welled in her eyes and her throat burned. Dead? Why?

"When we are safe, ah will tell ye all. But please, keep silent and follow close behind me..."

Lachlan did not have to finish the sentence for her to know he silently added the words "or we are dead a well."

They pushed on during the night and most of the next day, heading south toward England. Fortunately, as the day became late, they found an abandoned shack and rested until sundown eating dried beef and stale bread Lachlan had packed. If they rationed their food and water it may last three days. Not nearly the amount of time it would take them to cross onto English soil.

They continued to rest during the afternoons. Lachlan hunted squirrels and rabbits to keep them sustained. At night they resumed their trek until finally they reached a small village outside of Northumberland, settled in an abandoned cottage, and created new names. Teagan knew they wouldn't be safe forever, but they needed to rest before they purchased horses to continue on to London, seeking help from the Prince Regent. After all, Lachlan was the true heir to their father, The Duke of Tremont. Teagan prayed the prince would and could help them.

After settling in, Lachlan procured a job with the local blacksmith. They didn't need the coin, but in order to fit in with the local folks, Lachlan needed to work. As a young lad, when trying to escape from their father he would hide at the blacksmith's shop. Over the years, he learned the trade, never thinking he might need it someday to earn a living. Thank God he had. They also volunteered their services helping the locals hunt down the highwaymen terrorizing the small village. It went a long way in making the locals trust them. Newcomers were not well accepted or liked in this part of England. Nor were Scots. Something Teagan and Lachlan hoped to remedy to their advantage. If their father ever did find them, they would need trusted friends to help them escape him once again.

CHAPTER THREE

"Marissa. Marissa."

The voice of the patient startled Teagan awake from her perch on a wooden chair at his bedside just as nearby roosters crowed. "Easy. Relax," she said in a soothing voice as she dipped a clean cloth in cool water, squeezed out the excess and bathed his face, neck, and chest. Sometime during the night he'd developed a fever.

As she gently ran the cloth across his brow she said softly, "Who is Marissa? Is she yer wife, yer betrothed, or yer mistress?" *Does she possess yer heart?* For some unfathomable reason, Teagan didn't want his heart to belong to another woman. As she bathed his chest, lightly sprinkled with fair hair, her hands quivered and her breathing increased.

Who was this man? And why did his blue eyes plague her restless sleep? Having no answers to her questions, she placed the cloth in the chipped basin and went into the main room to mix a potent drink with healing herbs, hoping to get him to take some. She would do anything to keep him alive. If he died she would, for the remainder of her life, wonder about him. Think about him.

Back at his bedside, she inspected his wounds for infection. All looked much the same as yesterday. There was no rancid odor, which was a good sign. The fever was due to something else. Something she could not see.

"Good, ye are up," Teagan said to Lachlan when he entered the room rubbing his eyes. "Could ye help prop him up while ah get him tae drink?"

"Is that..." Her brother winced at the black concoction.

"Aye. And if ah recall ah saved your sorry arse with it more than once. Move him a little higher."

"Bossy this morning, aren't ya lass?"

"I'm trying tae save a life here. And ah added some of yer brandy tae help with the taste and the pain. If only we had laudanum."

"A stranger gets special treatment, but ah as yer brother didn't?"

She laughed. "Ah added brandy tae yers as weel, ah just didn't tell ye. Now steady while ah force his mouth open, hopefully without him biting my fingers off." Teagan knelt on the side of the bed and reached for his jaw, pulling it down. No luck, his teeth were mashed up tight. She tried to use her fingers to pry his mouth open. Didn't work. "Pinch his nose for me, that'll get him tae open his mouth. When ah pour it in and close his lips, keep his nose pinched until he swallows."

Lachlan did as she said and sure enough the injured man opened his mouth to gasp for air and she poured some medicine in and quickly closed his mouth, hoping he would swallow. He did, only to begin coughing and some of it sprayed her face. She grabbed a cloth and first wiped her face then his mouth and chin.

"Are you trying to kill me?" said her patient in a weak voice.

"Quite the contrary. We're trying tae save yer life." Teagan waited, hoping his good eye would open. As his lids began to flutter, she held her breath. One sky blue eye, foggy with fever and pain, stared at her. The other remained swollen shut."

"What is your name?" He breathed out.

Struck dumb, she stared wide-eyed at him. Every fiber of her being responded to his penetrating stare.

"Maggie," Lachlan admonished. "He asked yer name."

"Aye. Tis Maggie. And yers?" Mortified to find she still knelt on the bed, her knee pressed against his warm side, she quickly stepped off.

His eye closed and he inhaled deeply, making her fear he wouldn't answer.

"Sebastian Seabrook."

"Sebastian Seabrook," Lachlan said. "What brings ye tae Northumberland?"

"Is that where I am?"

"Aye."

"Tired."

"Who is Marissa? Ye spoke her name in yer sleep." Teagan said, ignoring her brother's knowing look. Unfortunately her patient fell back to sleep before he could tell her.

"Please dinnae tell me ye are jealous of this Marissa?"

Heat suffused her cheeks. "Not at all."

"Let me remind ye lass that ye didnae want tae save the mon. You wanted tae follow the highwaymen. Ye thought him dead at the river. Then you complained when ah tried tae bring him home."

"Ah changed my mind," Teagan huffed as she left the room to heat water for tea and make biscuits, leaving Mr. Seabrook in her brother's capable hands for now.

The next two days went on much the same, only Lachlan went to work at the blacksmith's shop.

CHAPTER FOUR

"I'M GETTING WORRIED," THOMAS SEABROOK, THE DUKE of Wentworth, said to his brothers-in-law, William Spencer, Earl of Bridgeton and Myles Fredrickson, Earl of Northborough. They sat in his study at Stony Cross Manor in Dover. "I expected to be without communication for a fortnight, but it has been longer and I'm worried for his safety. He had promised to send word immediately upon reaching Penelope's village. He should have arrived quite some time ago."

"Perhaps during his travels north he ran into my sister, Marissa, and her Captain while they eloped to Gretna Green," Myles said with a deep sigh. "I'll never understand how she can be in love with Sebastian one minute, well not minutes, but years, and then fall in love within a week with a Captain on leave she'd never set eyes on before."

"I can't answer about falling out of love, but I fell in love with Amelia almost immediately upon meeting her," Bridgeton said of his wife, Wentworth's sister.

"Yes, indeed, you did." Wentworth rose and moved to the sideboard to pour three glasses of amber liquid. After handing them out he downed his in one gulp, then refilled it, only he sipped it this time. "I have this uneasy feeling warning me I should search for him. That something is wrong." He moved to the window and pushed aside the drapes to stare out into the formal gardens bursting with summer color. "I ignored my uneasy intuition when I let him go." He snorted. "Not that I could have stopped him anyway once his mind was set. But I could have had Smythe assign someone to accompany him."

Wentworth closed his eyes as he finished his drink. He would never forgive himself if tragedy befell his brother. How could he? Even though their father had been dead four years now, he still reached out from his grave to do injustice to his family. If he'd kept his breeches buttoned up and didn't sleep with any doxy who glanced his way, they would not be in this precarious position. Sebastian wouldn't have gone off half-cocked and angry seeking a young girl claiming to be a sister to them. A natural born child to their womanizing father.

If this girl was their half-sister, Wentworth would welcome her with open arms. No child deserved to be alone in this world regardless of the circumstances surrounding their birth. According to the brief note she sent him, her mother recently passed due to a weak heart, and she was alone with very little money and nowhere to live. She didn't ask for help or money. She only told them her circumstances. Without having met her, Wentworth respected her already.

"I'll accompany you to find him," Myles said, pulling him out of his thoughts.

"As will I," Bridgeton added.

"I appreciate both of you offering, but Myles you must stay within a day's ride of London in case your sisters and mother need you. They rely on you, and I don't want to worry them about your safety after all they have been through recently. Not to mention you and Bella are newly married. Bridgeton, if you would be so inclined as to gather up Amelia and Olivia and stay here for a spell I would be forever indebted to you. With my wife expecting, I will rest easy knowing all my family are cared for."

Myles looked at him, a worried expression etched on his face. "After Sebastian has disappeared you don't honestly believe for one minute any of us will let you go alone, do you?"

"No. I will ask Amesbury." Wentworth, Myles, and Edward Worthington, Marquess of Amesbury had been friends since their days at Eton.

"When will you leave," Bridgeton asked, looking worried as well.

"First thing tomorrow morning If Amesbury arrives by then. I have several things I need to settle here before I leave." He pulled his pocket watch out and frowned at the time. "What is keeping Amesbury? I sent for him as well."

"Excuse me, Your Grace," the butler said as he knocked on the open door. "A message for you."

Thomas took the message, read it then excused the servant. "Amesbury won't be joining us. He's left for his country estate, something about a fire. Good Lord I hope all is well."

"Yes, indeed," Myles agreed.

"Let us hope no one was hurt, or worse," Bridgeton added.

"Do you think your cousin, Spencer, would accompany me? I believe you told me he was visiting with you for several days. And if he does, what about his family back in London?"

Bridgeton smiled. "He will jump at the chance to escape the endless female prattling that goes on in his house. After all that is why he arrived on my doorstep yesterday seeking peace. I will see to my grandmother, aunt, and cousins while he's away. It's high time they visited the country for a spell.

With Amelia and myself at your house, they can have my estate all to themselves. Which should please them."

"I'll send Spencer a note post haste. Meanwhile, thank you both for looking after my family while I'm away. You know I wouldn't go myself if I didn't have this constant feeling that something is amiss with Sebastian."

THAT EVENING as silence descended on the household and the rays from the full moon shined through the open windows, Wentworth held his wife close to his side. "Promise me you will take it easy while I'm gone."

Emma, curled against his side, her head resting on his chest said, "I promise. But do not fret, nothing is going to happen to me or our child. After all, this is not our first born. All was well with Hamilton's pregnancy, and I expect no less this time around. Find Sebastian and do not worry for us." She looked up at her husband and smiled. "I'm excited to spend time with Amelia and Olivia. Hamilton misses Olivia terribly since Amelia married Bridgeton and moved out."

"I will still worry. I hate to be apart from you for even a day. Have I told you today I love you?"

She gasped as his hand roamed down her back to cup her behind. "Yes. I believe you did this morning."

"Are you tired?" he asked as his need for her increased and hardened.

"Never tired for you, Your Grace."

WENTWORTH AND STUART SPENCER headed out at first light the next morning on horseback, deciding against traveling by coach as it would slow them down.

"Your message asking me to accompany you shocked me," Spencer said after they had put several miles behind them.

"I apologize for that. I admit you weren't my first choice, Amesbury was, but you were second. I need someone I can trust, and I trust you as we are family by way of Bridgeton marrying my sister."

"Even if we were not family, you can trust me. Hell, I spent most of my life keeping Bridgeton's family secrets. Some of his secrets have been revealed and some not, but none by my doing. However, it does free up space in my head for Seabrook family secrets."

"Seriously, he still has secrets?" Wentworth's hands tightened on the reins.

Spencer shifted uncomfortably in the saddle and looked away from him. "Fear not, Amelia knows all there is to know about his and his brother's past."

"That's a relief. For a minute there I thought I had to turn around and demand answers from him, then beat him to a bloody pulp."

"He is a most honorable man, you never have to worry about Amelia or her safety or future."

"I agree," Wentworth said. "I almost feel sorry for the way I treated him in the beginning when he first showed interest in Amelia." He grinned at his companion. "But not quite. We have become good friends, but I like to keep the husbands of my sisters questioning my inner thoughts."

Laughter shook Spencer's shoulder. "You are heartless, Your Grace, heartless."

"I beg to differ."

"Some days I still wish I were your brother-in-law," Spencer said, becoming serious. Something the gentleman almost never did.

"Have you gotten over your feelings for Bella?" Wentworth questioned. There was a time not long ago when both

Spencer and Myles vied for his sister, Isabella's affections. Myles won out. Truth be told, Bella had loved Myles for most of her life even though he knew Spencer held a small part of her heart as well.

"Yes and no. Yes, my heart has realized she belongs to another. But I miss her friendship. We shared much this past Season, and I find my days long without her to accompany me on my daily rides through the park."

"I heard from Myles that you acted like a school boy when you met his sister Caroline in the park one day."

Spencer chuckled. "Are there no secrets between you two? I admit I did. I was quite taken with her. Too bad she is too young for me. Not to mention she does not have her come out until next Season." He paused and shook his head. "Myles would never allow it."

"Why do you say that?" Wentworth asked. Young ladies of the *ton* married older gentlemen all the time.

"Just a hunch."

They traveled until the sun set that evening. The Inn they stayed at remembered Sebastian, so Wentworth was relieved to know he was at least alive and well when he'd stayed there.

CHAPTER FIVE

On the third day since the man—by the name of Sebastian Seabrook, stayed in her bed recovering from his attack—his fever broke and he asked for food. Teagan prepared a meat stew and served it with bread Lachlan bought from one of their neighbors. Unfortunately, their cabin had no oven to bake in, and Teagan didn't have the knowledge to make bread over an open flame.

Having helped Mr. Seabrook sit up a short time ago, she found it easy to spoon the stew into his mouth. "Ah don't dare give ye much. Yer stomach has been empty for several days now."

"I'm starving," he replied after he politely chewed his spoonful and opened his mouth for more.

Teagan laughed at the ridiculous way he looked. The eye that had been swollen shut was open a slit with a yellow and purple bruise beneath it. Bandages still covered most of his head, and her special black healing ointment ran down the side of his face covering his stitches. Her heart fluttered. A more handsome man she'd never seen. She needed to stop noticing things such as that. At least until she was convinced he could be trusted.

"I'm waiting," he said, his one good eye narrowing on her, causing heat to kiss her cheeks.

"Sorry." Try as she might, she could not keep her hand from trembling as the spoon carrying the stew approached his lips.

"Do I make you nervous? It is not my intention to do so."

"Mr. Seabrook," she huffed at him. "Ah assure ye ah'm not nervous."

"Sebastian please. There is no Mr. Seabrook."

She thought for a moment. "No Mr. Seabrook. Then "tis Lord Sebastian I presume?" She rose and curtsied with a smile.

"Should I be flattered or insulted by that curtsy?"

"Why flattered of course."

"Please don't treat me differently than you have. I'm the second son. It's my brother who's the duke."

"A duke." When her father dies Lachlan will also be a duke. "Is it difficult being the brother of a duke?"

The question brought a smile to his lips, and she melted back down into the chair.

"Not at all. I have never envied him. My father flaunted his mistresses and gambled the family fortune away. Poor Thomas inherited a mess and all our father's debts. For a year he stalled the creditors, swallowed his pride, and became a fortune-hunting duke. Fortunately for him and all of us in his family it ended well. He inherited money and a business from one of our father's childhood friends along with guardianship of his daughter."

"The answer tae his prayers ah suppose."

"You have no idea." He laughed. "He married his ward and they are happy, in love, and expecting baby number two."

"A fairytale made in heaven," Teagan replied with a heavy

heart. If only she could get that elusive fairytale ending. All she had to look forward to was being captured by her father and forced to marry, if not that brut of a man she'd wounded, then someone equally repulsive. A change of subject was needed so Sebastian didn't notice her sudden melancholy.

"How does yer arm and leg feel?" she asked as she spooned the last of the stew into his mouth. He raised his brows as he chewed as if to say, "you always ask questions then shove food in my mouth."

After he chewed he tested his arm and winced. "Hurts like a bugger. I beg your pardon for my language."

"May ah inspect yer leg?"

He nodded and took a deep breath, probably anticipating pain. Since he was still naked beneath the sheet, she carefully moved it off his leg but tugged and tucked it around his hips so as not to expose his man parts. Her cheeks already felt scorched, and she could only imagine what they would look like if she saw all his nakedness.

She unwrapped the bandages and inspected the area around the stitches. "It has good color, the skin around the stitches is less angry and there isnae much swelling anymore. Brice made ye a crutch to help you move around on until the wound heals. Ah dinnae want it opening up again. When yer ready, please let he or ah ken and we'll assist you."

The smile he sent her melted her bones. What was it about this man? Her body and mind had experienced strange and unusual happenings since bringing him to her home. True, when she and Lachlan had come across him lying half in the river and half on the banks, she believed him dead and didn't give him a care in the world. Even when she helped Lachlan move him and bring him here to her room and onto her bed, she still didn't think much about him. In her mind he was probably going to die.

While she had cleaned and bandaged his broken body,

something seeped into her skin through her fingertips. Whatever it was traveled throughout her body waking her up to her sensuality for the first time in her life. Those new awarenesses made her feel like a desirable woman. Something she'd never felt before.

"I don't think I'm ready to get up just yet," he hissed as she accidentally bumped his leg recovering him with the sheet.

"Just as weel. Ye need tae regain yer strength. Wouldnae want ye falling and injuring yerself in more ways." She couldn't help her hand from pushing the same lock of stray hair that kept creeping down in his eyes. "Ye should rest."

She should rest as well as she hadn't had much sleep since Sebastian arrived in their humble cottage. Unfortunately things needed tending to. At times like this she missed her pampered life in Scotland where she could rest a spell when the urge came over her. Albeit, that and her mother were the only things she missed. As for her father and Ian, she didn't care if she ever set eyes on them again as long as she lived. And for her and Lachlan's sake, she prayed she didn't. Nothing good would come of them coming face to face. More likely her and her brother's slow, torturous death would be the outcome.

Sebastian closed his eyes to rest, but his mind had other ideas. Since waking up in this room, he'd managed to piece together how he arrived here and he thanked God he was still alive. Those men who robbed and beat him, after he'd fallen off his mount and slid down an embankment bloody and hurt, had left him for dead. He owed his life to Maggie and Brice for bringing him here and mending his broken body. A frown creased his brow. The brother and sister lived like poor country folk, but they weren't your average country folk.

Even with their thick Scottish brogue they spoke like the privileged gentry. Something was not right about this. The only thing he knew for certain was they meant him no harm. Meanwhile, he would heal and hopefully find out the truth about them.

Maggie, he grinned and winced at the pain radiating up his face. Beautiful Maggie. The first time he glimpsed her gorgeous red hair cascading down around her shoulders, he'd believed he'd gone to heaven and she his angel of mercy. What an utterly pleasant surprise to find out he lived and she —a living, breathing woman, cared for him with gentle, knowing hands. The emerald green of her eyes changed with her fluctuating emotions. When she concentrated on his injuries, they darkened with worry and concern. During their easy conversation of just minutes ago, they lightened and sparkled with amusement.

When she'd leaned over his naked body, clad only with a light sheet, and her breast brushed his thigh as she examined his leg, he'd nearly groaned. And he wondered if she'd noticed something stirring to life beneath the sheets. Thank God she took that moment to touch his injured leg causing him unbearable pain, which squashed his rising desire.

Something about Maggie called to his inner self. It didn't matter that he believed she wasn't who she said she was. If she hid something, Sebastian didn't believe for a minute it was bad. Nothing about her could be truly evil. She emanated such innocence and genuine kindness—he knew without a doubt, a true beautiful soul lived within her.

How could he be thinking about his attraction to his savior when he still needed to find his half-sister? He scolded himself. She had sounded desperate in her letter, and he worried about what she had omitted in her correspondence.

They all believed there were things she refused to say or couldn't say. Was she starving? She hinted at being an age of around sixteen or seventeen. Was there a man trying to coerce her into giving him her innocence in return for shelter and food?

If only he weren't injured, he could purchase a horse and ride today. Then his insides stilled. There were two problems with that. His body was in need of healing and he had no funds. Perhaps Maggie would write to Wentworth for him even though his pride would need to be swallowed. He'd let his family down and he hated it. Hated the sick feeling in the pit of his stomach for failing to find Penelope.

"Ah thought ye were resting," Maggie said with a soft concerned voice. The cadence of it soothed his worried mind.

"May I ask something of you?"

She must have noticed his seriousness because she approached the bedside and took his hand, the one belonging to his unbroken arm, in her small callused ones. "Anything."

"I need to send word to my family. They must be worried."

Immediately, she let go of his hand. "Oh my God, how could ah havenae thought about yer family?" She rushed from the room, came back with her face flushed and her hair in disarray, and his heart fluttered with longing. After setting down parchment, ink, and quill on a small chest of drawers with missing knobs, she stood ready.

"You didn't know my identity until today, so don't be upset. There was nothing you could do," Sebastian said, trying to ease her worried look and he succeeded. Only now she looked at him with a smile and expectant eyes. Swallowing, he hoped to ease the sudden dryness in his throat, and he began to tell her what he wanted put in the missive.

"Dear Wentworth, I have not found Penelope. I am fine, but my horse and I got caught in a terrible storm and got lost.

I was unfortunately injured. A brother and sister just outside of Northumberland have taken me in until I heal. Please do not worry about me, but I am concerned about Penelope. Perhaps you should seek Mr. Smythe's help. I hope this letter finds you and our family well. Your brother, Sebastian."

"Is that all?" Maggie asked with a frown. "Should ye nae tell them how extensive yer injuries are? And that ye were accosted and robbed and left for dead by highwaymen?"

"No. I don't want to worry my family when they have other things to concern themselves with. My sisters, Bella and Amelia, both newly married had some tragedy in their lives, they don't need any more stress upsetting them. My brother's wife is increasing with their second babe and Emma needn't concern herself with anything but her and the babe's health. And if I know my brother, he will leave immediately for here or to find Penelope. Hopefully to find Penelope."

"If ah may be so bold to ask, who is Penelope?"

"I beg your pardon. She is claiming to be our father's natural born daughter. I was traveling to her and bringing her to my family's country estate in hopes of finding out the truth. I let my family and her down."

"Ye didnae let her down. Ye tried yer best. "Tis nae yer fault ye were accosted by highwaymen. And if her claim turns out tae be true, she will be a lucky lady indeed tae have found such a loving family as yers."

Sebastian heard the sorrow in her voice, and he wondered about her family other than her brother. The haunted look in her eyes just now made his heart ache for her. Something happened to scar her deeply. "Tell me about your family?"

"There is nothing tae tell." Her eyes darted away from his. He knew deep inside she lied to him. Perhaps when she needed a friend to talk to, she would share.

"May I ask one more question?" Her eyes stayed diverted from his and he missed the contact.

"Yes."

"Who is Marissa?"

Witnessing Maggie blush softened the shock of hearing Marissa's name spoken out loud. Then he exhaled and closed his eyes, briefly acknowledging the sudden but quick stab to his heart. Perhaps he was getting over her quicker than he thought because his heart only hurt for a moment, and he breathed easier. "She is my brother's best friend, the Earl of Northborough's sister. The earl is also married to my sister, Bella. Marissa and I practically grew up together. Our two families were and are very close." He paused, trying to find the right words to make him not look like a bloody arse.

"We were not betrothed, but it was expected we would marry. I don't know what I was waiting for? Perhaps I wasn't truly convinced we would suit one another as husband and wife or that I loved her in that way. One week before I left home, she ran off to Gretna Green with a captain she'd only recently met. Obviously she arrived to the same conclusion I had."

"I'm sorry," Maggie whispered as she took his hand. "Are ye worried for her running off with this captain she just met?"

"No. Marissa might have just met him, but I went to Eton with him. He's a second son like me, and we were quite close during are education years. Lost touch when he entered His Majesty's Army, but I have no qualms that he will take good and loving care of Marissa. They make a fine couple. Of course when they return from Scotland, he'll have Northborough to answer to."

"Is Lord Northborough quick tae temper?"

Sebastian laughed, then gasped in pain as his laughter shook his whole body, jarring his leg and arm. "No. Myles, as he prefers to be called by his friends, is easy going, charming and witty. If Marissa is happy, he will be ecstatic. He, along with my brother, want love matches for their siblings."

Maggie frowned and looked wishful. "Love matches. If only my pa—" Her hand flew to her mouth and her eyes widened in shock.

"I thought your mother and father were dead?" Sebastian asked, knowing he'd caught her in a lie. Would she trust him enough to tell him the truth?

"They are." She recovered fast. "Ah meant tae say, when my paw were alive he dinnae care if ah found love. He only wanted me tae marry someone who could provide for me and any children we were blessed tae conceive. He gave my maw little say in the matter. As for my brother, they wanted him tae marry the mean spirited daughter of a neighboring wealthy estate owner." Her brows drew together. "He refused."

"Why?"

She released his hand, looking startled to realize she still held it. "No more questions please. If ye'll excuse me, I'll leave ye tae rest and go find Brice and hand him yer letter. He'll need tae find someone tae take it tae yer family."

"Wait." He didn't know why he reached out to her, but he didn't want to be alone with his thoughts even though he was exhausted and had trouble keeping his eyes open. "Stay."

She shook her head. "Ah'm sorry, ah cannae."

As he closed his eyes and felt the pull of sleep, he wondered once again what secrets she hid. Would he ever have the privilege of knowing? Was Maggie even her true name?

ON HER WAY TO find her brother, Teagan chastised herself for letting her guard down with Sebastian. Just because he was English didn't mean her father didn't send him? He could still be their enemy. She would have to be more careful in the future not to be swayed by his good looks and charm.

"Brice," Maggie called as she stood in the doorway of the blacksmith shop.

He rushed to the door and pulled her outside. "What are ye doing here? Are ye daft, ye left him alone?"

"He asked me tae write a letter tae his family. His name is Sebastian Seabrook, and his brother is the Duke of Wentworth." She paused to catch her breath. "Do ye think he is making it up? That he is just trying to worm his way into our trust so we will let our guard down? Or can we believe him? His story is plausible. Should we send the letter?"

Lachlan pulled her along with him. She knew he wanted to get them out of the prying eyes and ears of several town folks. The residents of this small town were still leery of them, being Scottish and all. One of the main reasons he'd left his kilt at home and wore English clothing. Another being he didn't want to stand out in case his father's men caught up with him. Dressing as the English did would enable them to blend in with the townsfolk.

"What did ye tell him?"

"Ah said ye would find someone tae deliver the missive."

"We cannae send it," Lachlan said with a frown. "Even if he is telling the truth, we cannae have his family members coming into our home. In case ye havenae noticed, his eyes follow our every move. He has a suspicious nature. Ah think he suspects we are nae who we say we are. And if his brother, the duke, arrives and he shares his beliefs, what then?"

"This could be tae our advantage. Surely the duke must have the ear of the prince. He could help us?" By the expression on her brother's face, she'd not convinced him. "Ah finally believe he is no threat to us, and ye willnae help him?

"Nay. Give me the letter?"

Teagan regrettably handed over the sealed letter. She

didn't believe Sebastian or his brother—if they found out the truth about them—would notify their father. Not if they told him how he wanted Lachlan dead and possibly her as well.

After leaving her brother, she walked slowly home, pondering how outlandish their life had become. And if she would ever feel safe or be free again?

When she arrived home she had to be assured she had total privacy, so she tiptoed to the doorway and her breath stopped at the sight before her. Sebastian had unwrapped his bandages on his head and she saw for the first time his lovely blond hair.

Immediately she wanted to run her fingers through it in the worst way. Shaking her head, she left the room to quickly disrobe, remove her dirty dress and chemise, and put on her only other clean piece of clothing, another chemise. After washing the discarded items and several other pieces of clothing, she hung them on a rope tied between two trees that Lachlan had created.

Now she set to work making another stew for several meals to come. How she missed the meals served at Murray Castle. Why had she never appreciated the family's servants or the cook and kitchen staff? One of several things she'd learned on this forced adventure was to be forever grateful for the help of servants. If she ever saw her home again, she would make time to thank each and every member of the staff. And never take them for granted again. She had not been unkind to any of them but had not gone out of her way to be kind either.

She realized, now that she handled everything, that servants had a thankless job. And she felt sorry for them being born poor and of the lower classes. Teagan would admit she had been somewhat a spoiled child when younger. Her mother had doted over her endlessly, dressing her in extravagant clothing and parading her around the village. Silent tears leaked from her eyes at the thought of her strong but kind-hearted mother. Never could she ever understand what her mother saw in her father.

Her father had never shown any interest in Teagan. He thought females were useless, except for overseeing the household and warming a man's bed at night. And yes, for baring sons. Many sons. He'd never *not* shown his disappointment in her being a girl.

But if her father valued sons over daughters, why had he always been displeased with Lachlan? No. More than displeased, almost as though he hated him. Lachlan didn't deserve his father's hatred. He was the first born son.

Why was her younger brother by a year so revered by their father? Because surely, Ian was not the better choice to run an estate? He took after their father, mean-spirited, tight-fisted, and demanding while Lachlan took after Mother. No doubt that being the reason their father bonded with Ian and wanted him to inherit. Or more likely Ian was the way he was because of Father. Father trained him from the time he left the cradle.

If only things had been different and their mother still lived. When Mother had wed Father, she brought the wealth into the Murray coffers. From what Teagan had been told, the castle was in disrepair until her mother's dowry, which had been much more substantial than most. It must have been if they never lacked for coin over the years.

Rumors had been whispered since she was a little girl. Rumors about her mother carrying Lachlan and her before the nuptials were exchanged. Her parents had married quickly, there wasn't even time for a hand-fasting. Even if there was truth to this, why would Father not like them? To her limited knowledge about married people, this type of hurried ceremony happened quite often.

Wiping away her tears as she chopped up vegetables for a

stew, she willed herself to stop crying as the tears wouldn't change anything. Her mother was still dead. And she found it unfortunate her brother wouldn't send the letter to the Duke. Deep down inside she believed he would help them. Sebastian made him sound like a kind, honorable, and caring man.

How could anyone who knew their plight, not want to help them? A sudden bang and shattering glass from the bedroom had her wiping her hands and running into the room. Sebastian stood, pain etched on his face, his teeth clenched.

"Bloody hell. I'm sorry. Look at the mess I've created. I only wanted to see if I could get up.

"Do nae fret." Teagan reached for him because he looked as though he would topple any moment. Which he did, falling back onto the bed and taking her with him. As she fell on top of him, he yelled in pain.

"Ah'm sorry," she said as she struggled to get up.

"No. Don't move. Give me a moment to breathe through the pain."

Teagan stilled. The only thing she did was lift her head and look into his mesmerizing blue eyes. Both of which were open now. Even though they radiated discomfort, they took her breath away with their intensity. "Forgive me, ah only meant tae help ye."

"You did. Without you I may have landed on the floor." His chest rose and fell, and his heart beat fast beneath her chest. Strange, her heart beat rapidly as well.

She swallowed hard because she realized he was totally naked beneath her. When she entered the room she had panicked so at seeing him standing and swaying that she didn't notice his unclothed state. Nor hers as she wore only a chemise as her clothing dried. Now as she lay on top of him, she felt every muscle, bone, and dip in his body. As well as his swollen member pushing against her stomach.

"May ah get up now?" she said in a near whisper as all the air had escaped from her lungs.

"Must you?" His one free arm curled around her and landed softly against her back. The warmth from his large hand settled deep within her bones. Odd how this near stranger affected her so. He made her long for things her body seemed to understand but not her mind. Oh, she knew what happened between a man and women sexually, but to experience it, was another matter entirely. She'd never even kissed a man, never mind got this close. A heat burned in her belly and she felt wet down below. Between her thighs.

"Ah must. If La...Brice found me thus."

It took all her willpower to divert her eyes from his soul searching ones and rise off his body. As her unsteady feet landed on the ground she looked back, gasped, and covered her mouth with her hand. She'd seen penises of old and sick men, and the one time with MacPherson, but nothing she'd ever seen prepared her for what Sebastian had between his legs. His shaft was thick and long and not unpleasant to look at.

As she stared at it she swore it grew in length and girth. "Ah'm sorry."

"No. Forgive me," he said as he struggled to pull the sheet over him to no avail. "It appears I need some help." His cheeks were bright red with embarrassment.

All her focus was on his face as she gently tugged the sheet from beneath him and covered his waist. "Ah must ask my brother for some clothing for ye as we cut yers off. Excuse me," she mumbled, trying to keep herself in control. "Ah have things tae attend tae."

As she left the room and draped the fabric across the door opening, she covered her pounding heart with one hand and her heated cheek with the other. "Deep breaths, deep even breaths," she told herself, hoping to calm the rapid beat of her heart and the vibrations in her body. How had that happened? One minute she was saving him from toppling over and hurting himself and the next she landed on top of his hard, naked body. A body that would be forever remembered in her mind. Even if he turned out to be their enemy, she would remember. Although she prayed he was not in their father's employ.

Going back to preparing the meal, she took extra careful precautions chopping vegetables as her hands trembled still. After setting everything in the cast-iron kettle on the open flame in the small stone fireplace, she tidied up the cabin even though she'd cleaned early that morning.

All she knew was she needed something to keep her occupied until Lachlan returned from work. Distance between her and Sebastian would be wise. Over the course of the past several years she recognized when a man lusted after her, and she'd witnessed that same lust shining from Sebastian's midnight blue eyes.

Even though she had never lusted after a man before, she had experienced it then. She had stared at his slightly parted lips and wanted so desperately for him to kiss her. For his mouth to crush hers in a kiss worthy of a swooning.

Of course, Sebastian may lust after her now, but when he found out about their deception, he would feel differently. Possibly even hate her. Unless he had deceptions of his own. Her hand palmed the pain in her chest at the idea of him hating her. Why had Lachlan insisted they lie? Yes, she knew the reasons why, but her female intuition told her he would prove an ally in their fight with their father. And they needed all the help they could receive to stay hidden and alive. God forbid their father found them, they would need more than luck or Sebastian. They would need an army of loyal men. An army they didn't have, nor would.

CHAPTER SIX

"OH, GOOD, YE'R HOME," TEAGAN SAID TO LACHLAN AS HE walked through the door carrying a small basket. "What have we here?"

"Eggs. Mrs. Nagle stopped me on my way home from work and offered them tae us." He placed the small basket on the round wooden table. "My mouth's been watering for them the entire walk here."

"Ah'll make us eggs in the morning."

"Why nae dinner?" Lachlan said, not bothering to hide his excitement about the eggs. "'Tis been ages since we had them."

"Ah made stew for dinner."

"Again?"

Teagan swung around, hands on hips and faced him. "What else would ye have me make? That and eggs is about all ah ken how. Dinnae forget we grew up with cooks. If it wasnae for my curiosity when ah was younger and spending hours watching the cook in the kitchen, ah wouldnae even ken how tae do this."

SEEING his sister's frustration had Lachlan rethinking the eggs for dinner. "Ah'm sorry. Ye are right. Ye are doing the best ye can under the circumstances. We both are." It was true they were. But, bloody hell, he was tired from restless sleepless nights and watching over his shoulder every minute of every day. He could not be caught unawares.

If anything happened to him, what would become of Teagan? He would give his life to keep her safe, but if he did, she would be much worse off than she was now.

"How is yer patient today?" Did his eyes deceive him or did she just blush and advert her gaze.

"He tried tae get out of bed. Actually he succeeded, only tae call for help. Fortunately ah was able tae assist him back tae bed without any damage done."

"Hmmm." Lachlan studied her face once again and found the color even pinker. What had happened while he was gone? It wasn't proper for her to be with this man all day while he worked, but what choice did they have?

"Was he nae naked?"

More color suffused her cheeks. "Aye, and that reminds me, do ye have extra clothing for him? I cannae verra weel be expected tae take care of an unclothed mon. Ye should have seen..." Her voice abruptly stopped, her hand covered her mouth, and her eyes widened in shock.

"Seen what exactly?" He knew he was embarrassing her more by his question.

"Ye verra weel ken what and ah'll nae be saying it," she huffed. "Please at least give him some trews tae wear so ah can help him without closing my eyes."

He chuckled. He couldn't help himself.

"Ye think this funny?" She exhaled loudly.

"Nae at all. Ah should be scandalized letting my young,

unmarried, chaste sister take care of a virile mon of English gentry alone." He waved his arm around. "What choice do ah have, ah must work tae appear tae the townsfolk that we are one of them. That even if Paw's mon find their way tae this remote village, the good folks here will stand behind us."

"Ah must apologize brother. Ah grow wearier as each day passes. Ah wish they would find us and get our fate done with."

Lachlan gasped. "How can ye say that? Nae with that giant of a mon Paw has given ye tae. Ah mon ah'm quite convinced will beat ye until ye submit tae him in all things. Beat ye until ye no longer resemble the woman ye are."

"Dinnae ye think ah ken this?" She spun around and paced the small room. "Living as we are gives us our freedom, but what else?"

"Teagan, lower yer voice." Lachlan nodded his head towards the fabric, the only barrier between them and him.

"Several times today ah almost called ye by yer true name. One of these times ah'm afraid ah will."

"Shhhh." Lachlan put his finger to his lips. "Ah heard something. Is he awake?"

"He wasnae the last time ah checked," she replied as she moved silently to the curtain and moved it aside just enough to peer inside. She jumped back and gasped.

"What is it," Lachlan asked as he joined her at the partition to the rooms. "Weel, weel, have ye been listening?"

Lachlan wasn't surprised to find Sebastian standing at the opening, one side of his body leaning heavily on the makeshift wooden crutch. What did surprise him was that three days after the man was beaten and left for dead, he was standing, albeit wincing in pain, but standing with an injured leg and broken arm. The other thing that pleased him was he had wrapped a sheet around his waist. Good man.

"My most sincere apologies for overhearing. I needed to

get up and stretch my cramped muscles. I'm not used to such idleness. I was going crazy."

"Would ye care tae sit by the fire?" Teagan asked as she gestured to a small wooden chair.

"I would, but it might be difficult getting there."

"My brother will assist ye." She tilted her head and smiled at Lachlan, no doubt willing him to argue with her. Well, he would not. Instead, he wrapped his arm under the man's shoulder of his uninjured arm and helped him move the several paces to the chair. After settling him on the edge of the seat he stepped back, arms across his chest, and stared down. "So tell me what ye heard?"

Lachlan thought better of the man because he actually blushed and looked uncomfortable. "I know you gave me false names, but I don't have a clue as to why?"

Lachlan sensed Teagan was going to speak. He placed his hand on her arm to stop her. "Let me."

"Ye cannae be serious in planning to trust him?" Teagan said. Suddenly the room seemed to close in around her and she couldn't get air into her lungs. Doubt assaulted her from all angles and she actually felt sorry for the stranger and guilty at her thoughts. "We dinnae ken for sure..."

"We can trust him. I believe it in here." Lachlan hit his chest with his fist.

"Since when?"

"Since now." Lachlan paced the room, every nerve in his body screaming. Could they trust this man? Yes, they saved his life, but that didn't mean money or something else could sway him to betray them if he had the chance. Their father could be very convincing. He was also not opposed to torture to get his way. Could he put this man's life in jeopardy by confiding in him?

Feeling as though he had no choice in the matter, he told the whole sordid tale of how and why they came to be in England. Teagan added her side of the story when necessary.

Now Lachlan waited as Sebastian, as he preferred to be called, digested the information and said something, anything, to break the silence and tension plaguing the small room.

"I thought my father was a bastard but not compared to yours. And I want you to know my family is not without scandal. So I'm not shocked by your words. In fact, I'm quite certain you shall get the help you seek from the prince." He paused and used his good hand to rub the knee of his injured leg. "Have you sent word yet?"

That was the problem. Lachlan didn't trust it not to fall into the wrong hands. Who could he trust to get his letter safely to the prince? For all he knew his father had men watching them now.

"I WOULD GLADLY DELIVER it myself if I could." Sebastian would as soon as he healed, but it could take another sennight before he could ride a horse, or even longer. Perhaps he could still convince them to send a missive to London. God knew how long they would be safe here so close to the Scottish border.

As he contemplated their dire situation, his eyes sought out Maggie...Teagan. He much preferred Teagan. Maggie had never seemed right and now he knew why.

She stood in front of the fire, stirring the stew while using her free hand to hold a shawl across her shoulders in hopes of modesty. He did not know why she dressed only in a chemise, which did little, even with the shawl, to hide what lay beneath. Her body was thinner than most of the ladies in London, but that didn't mean she didn't have curves where curves were wanted. He'd felt them first hand when she lay on top of him. In fact, he'd felt every muscle, bone, and cushion in her body.

Bloody hell, if Lachlan looked at him now he'd likely throw his sorry arse out into the cold—injured and all. He'd never had trouble controlling his baser needs around women, even Marissa. What was it about Teagan?

Marissa never caused his blood to boil and his member to twitch like Teagan did. What did that say about him? Lachlan should be wary. Not for the reasons he explained but for very serious ones pertaining to his lust for his sister. Not that he planned on acting on that lust. At least he would try not to.

If he was not mistaken, Teagan experienced lust herself for him as well. He'd witnessed it in her compelling green eyes while their bodies were connected. Swore, he'd caught a whiff of her arousal as well.

Was this what it was like to ache for someone and not know if you'd ever have her? Ever hold her close to your heart? If so, he'd like to pass on the whole emotional experience.

As far as Lachlan explained, Teagan was promised to some brute of a man by the name of MacPherson who tried to rape and beat her. Christ, what kind of father allowed that?

Now he had two women he wanted to save. His half-sister and this near stranger who called to his heart, body, and soul. Teagan Murray—Lady Teagan Murray. If they had met under normal circumstances, would they have been drawn to each other? Waltzed at a ball and made small talk over tea. He hoped so.

"Do you have an escape plan when and if they find you?" He prayed they did.

"Aye and nay," Teagan answered as she pulled the shawl together, and he forced his eyes on her face instead of the indented curve of her slim waist illuminated by the firelight.

"We have hidden a change of clothing, provisions and coin safely in the forest. Honestly, we should have left here weeks ago."

"Aye, we should have, but then who would have saved Sebastian's life," Lachlan said, continuing to walk the small room. "Things happen for a reason. We were meant tae save ye."

"I am most grateful that you did. But now that I'm well enough, you two should travel to my brother in Dover. He will see you sheltered and safely to London and Whitehall for an audience with the prince." He took a deep breath and rubbed the constant cramp in his good leg. Damn but it was awkward sitting with his other leg bandaged and unable to bend. "When you arrive, if you do before my letter, have him send a carriage for me."

Teagan gasped. "Ah will nae leave ye. Ye are nae strong enough. Besides, how will ye eat? Ye cannae even make it ten feet without assistance."

"As much as ah am anxious tae leave and be on the road, ah agree with the lass. We cannae leave ye behind."

"Are you positive your father sent his men after you?"

"Nae completely," Lachlan said as he stopped in front of the fireplace and smelled the stew. "But ah ken him, and besides MacPherson would have. The lass did a number on him, and it would be a matter of pride and wounded monhood, so he would. And ah dinnae believe for a moment, he means tae spare her life. He will marry her and kill her on the same night."

Tremors ran through Sebastian's body at the thought of beautiful, innocent Teagan dead at the hands of the man meant to protect and care for her. Images of her battered and broken body had him gasping for air. "We cannot let that happen. Lachlan, you cannot let it happen. You must leave tonight. Do not worry about me. You need to protect your sister at all costs. My body is healing more every day and getting stronger. You must leave and not worry about me."

IF TEAGAN HAD any doubts about Sebastian and the truth to his story, after his speech, she no longer did. He was all that was good and noble.

"Ah...we will nae leave ye here. Besides, Lachlan and ah are going out tonight scouting for the highwaymen who did this tae you."

"You are what?" Sebastian said with a shocked expression, which then turned to worry.

"Teagan and ah have been hunting them, trying tae get the townsfolk tae trust us. If our paw comes looking for us, we need the good people here tae think of us as one of them. Likewise, the highwaymen have been wreaking havoc and stealing from folks who can hardly afford tae lose a shilling, never mind a week's or month's wages."

"But surely you will not risk the life of your sister? Cannot some of the menfolk around here go out with you?"

"Aye and nay. Ah won't risk another's life if ah come upon my paw's mon while hunting the bandits." Lachlan looked from Sebastian to Teagan and back with a grin. "Trust me, she can handle herself quite weel. As soon as the sun sets we will be going."

Teagan didn't want to express to her brother her insides were aquiver with worry that something would go wrong this evening.

When the sun set and they had Sebastian settled into bed, they rode out on borrowed mounts from the blacksmith, with Teagan dressed in Lachlan's clothing and her fiery red hair tucked into a hat. They decided long ago that she needed the disguise not only from their father's men, but from the highwaymen as well. Teagan's insides shook at the thought of her female identity becoming known.

For several hours they traveled the dirt roads and ducked into the forest, hoping to come upon the highwaymen's camp. Once again they were stumped as to where the men were. It was as though they didn't exist except when they went on the attack. How could that be? They had to be somewhere close by. They had to have shelter somewhere near.

Lachlan led the way home at a slow pace. Teagan didn't mind as her body was bone weary. And her horse equally so. As they approached their small cabin, her horse shied away as did Lachlan's.

"What is it?" she asked in a whisper?

"I dinnae ken. Follow me," he mouthed as he backed his horse up into the cover of the woods. "Something is verra wrong. Stay here while ah go and see."

Teagan didn't want to wait, but she did. She dismounted and held the reins to both horses as Lachlan slithered into the night.

LACHLAN, having been good at sneaking out of his home as a child and then as an adult to get away from his father, used those skills now to creep up to the cabin silently. He flattened himself against the wall, then crouched down low and peeked into the bedroom window, hoping to find Sebastian well and safe.

"Bloody hell," he muttered under his breath. Sebastian was gone. And then he heard voices coming from the main room. He made his way silently to the other side of the cabin and peered into the only other window, and his heart stopped.

Sebastian was tied up to a wooden chair and being questioned by Ian. What the bloody hell was his brother doing here? As if he didn't know?

"Where are they?" asked Ian right before he backhanded Sebastian across the face, nearly knocking the man and chair over.

"I don't know who you mean. I was attacked by high-waymen and sought shelter at this abandoned shack a sennight ago. There is no one here but me. The people you seek must have left."

"I dinnae believe ye." Ian paced the room, his features in a rage as he pointed to two of his father's henchmen. "Go, search the woods. They must be hiding like the cowards they are."

Lachlan took off at a dead run to reach Teagan. "Quick. We must be off. They are coming tae search the woods. We can hide at the blacksmith's shop. They willnae think tae look there."

Once they were safe inside the blacksmith's shop with the horses as well, Lachlan breathed his first deep breath in forever.

"They have Sebastian tied tae a chair and when Ian doesnae like his answers, he beats him."

"Our brother is here? Why him?"

"I dinnae rightly ken. Perhaps Paw thought it was his duty tae hunt us down and kill us."

"Who is there?" a deep voice called out in the dark.

"George, it is ah, Brice. My sister and ah need yer help."

Lachlan explained the situation to George, while apologizing for the untruths.

"That's quite a story. I knew you were not who you said, but I knew you were a good man and that's all I needed to know."

"Can we stay here and rest a spell?"

"Stay as long as you like. I'll send the misses down with some food."

"Thank ye for yer kindness," Teagan said to the nice man.

After a sleepless night in the blacksmith's barn, Lachlan and Teagan decided to ride out to the small cottage and try to make a deal with Ian.

Just as they were leaving, George came into the barn to start his day. When he understood what they planned he said, "You cannot go. From what you explained last night, your brother will kill you on sight, Brice...I mean Lachlan. Then who will keep your sister safe? For surely you don't think this Lord Sebastian is up to the task with his broken arm and injured leg."

"Bloody hell," Lachlan exclaimed. "Everything ye say is true. But how can ah stand back and let the Englishmon be beaten, protecting Teagan and myself?"

"Well, I believe your answer just arrive," George said.

Lachlan's jaw dropped when ten locals armed with swords and pistols entered the barn. The resident leading the pack was a Mr. David Johnson, the local barkeep. A burly man to be sure. His fist was the size of a ham and his head, Lachlan didn't have the words to describe the size of the man's head. Nor did he care. He was too touched that these folks were willing to risk their lives to help two Scottish strangers.

"Thank ye for coming here this morning. But before ye risk everything tae help my sister and ah, ye need tae ken the truth of what awaits." Lachlan proceeded to explain the dire situation at the cottage and what transpired back in Scotland. These brave men deserved nothing less than the absolute truth. His father's hatred of him made defending him risky. When describing his father, he said he was laird of Murray Castle. He left out the part of him being a duke.

"George explained it all and we are behind you and your sister. You may have only lived here a short time, but you have proven yourself with your pursuit of the highwaymen and helping to keep our small community safe," Johnson said. "Nothing you say can keep us from helping." He looked around the barn and grinned. "Besides, when do we get the chance to kick some Scottish arses?"

Loud roars assaulted Lachlan's ears and he joined in with the hollering. He took no offense about the Scottish remark. Living on the border, these men probably had many reasons to hate the Scots. All that mattered was they didn't hate Teagan and him. No, sir, they were defending them.

Shortly after that conversation they came up with a plan. Several of the men would approach the cottage, pretending upon a visit to Sebastian. They would try to convince Ian and his men to go outside by saying they just saw Lachlan and Teagan riding up the road towards the cottage.

Hopefully, when all the men were outside, the rest of the town's folk, along with Lachlan, would attack them. Lachlan said he didn't care who lived or died, with one exception, his brother was to be unharmed but detained with restraints.

Lachlan wanted answers. Answers his brother would supply.

"Teagan will ride with us, but stay hidden in the woods with a guard."

"Why?" she queried.

"Because ah willnae have ye hurt or kidnapped and dragged back tae Scotland tae marry that brut Paw picked out for ye."

"Ah can take care of myself," she declared with her chin held up high.

"Teagan," Lachlan began in a calm voice. "Ah ken ye can. But this is tae dangerous. Paw could have mon in the woods waiting tae attack us. If ah leave ye alone, God only kens what might happen. Between ye and the one guard, ah know if anyone has the unfortunate luck of happening upon ye, he'll likely regret it for the rest of his life. Such as it will be with him maimed and all."

"Fine." Teagan re-tucked her long hair into the borrowed cap. "Ah hope our dear brother, Ian, prayed for his soul tae God today."

CHAPTER SEVEN

TEAGAN COULD HARDLY BELIEVE WHAT TRANSPIRED outside the small cottage. Ian and his four men were easily overtaken. The minute all five men were bound, Teagan exited the woods at a run and didn't stop until she stood and faced her brother. "From this moment on, ye are no longer my brother. Go back tae Paw and tell him tae forget about Lachlan and me. We will never set foot on Scottish soil until he rots beneath the earth, in hell, where he belongs. And ye." She punched him in the chest. "Ye are a disgrace tae our family name. I hope tae never look on yer face again."

The glare of hatred in her brother's eyes caused her heart to pause mid-beat.

"How about ah share a little secret with ye," Ian said with a smirk. "Paw is nae yer Paw. Mother was a whore and carried another mon's twins in her belly. She spread her legs for a married mon and let him spill his seed inside her. So ye see, ye have no Paw. My Paw hated Maw and he hates ye and Lachlan."

Teagan couldn't breathe, her lungs constricted refusing to let air in. The world spun and she dropped to her knees. So the part about Mother being with child before the wedding was true. But never had she heard so much as a whisper that the father was anyone other than the duke. And now to find out she had a real father out there somewhere shocked her to the core.

Finally she gasped air, stood, and hurried inside the cottage, whipping tears away from her face. She didn't want Sebastian to see her weeping. After she was convinced he was unharmed there would be time to ponder whether the words Ian spoke about her father were true. And did Lachlan know?

"Oh, God," she cried as her hands covered her mouth to stifle her screams. The sight of Sebastian's bloody face startled her even though Lachlan had said he was being beaten. Never did she imagine it to be so bad.

"Ah'm here." She approached Sebastian, knelt on the floor behind him, and tried to untie the rope wrapped around his chest and arms. She prayed the bone in his arm wasn't re-broken. Her fingers shook so badly she did more harm than good. "Ah need a knife." She rose and rummaged through a drawer until her trembling fingers found what she sought. "Dinnae move." Teagan placed the sharp blade of the knife against the ropes, inhaled and exhaled hoping to steady her fingers. It wouldn't be good if she cut Sebastian while trying to free him. Before she slipped the knife beneath the rope, she dropped it and it hit the floor with a loud thud. "Sorry. My fingers refuse tae work."

"Take your time. I'm not going anywhere anytime soon," Sebastian said with a slur to his words. Making her even more nervous. How badly was he hurt? Had Ian made his skull fracture worse?

Closing her eyes, she envisioned the warmth of the sun calming her and regulating her breathing. When she opened her eyes, she made quick work of cutting the rope around Sebastian's body and ankles, freeing him.

"Do ye think, with my help, we can get ye into bed?"

"Only one way to find out."

Teagan carefully wrapped her arm around him and used all her strength to help him stand.

"Damn," he swore. "Even the hair on top of my head hurts."

"Ah'm sorry." Teagan fought the renewed tears burning her eyes and throat. There would be time later to have a good cry for Sebastian and the guilt eating her insides at putting him in danger.

"Sorry for what?"

"Cannae explain now. Ye'r heavy."

The two of them struggled but finally got Sebastian in bed. She inspected his leg and arm first. Fortunately the stitches on his leg and face held up and the bone in his arm lined up. Thank God for that. "Ah'll be right back."

Once she found herself in the safety of the outer room, her shoulders rolled forward, her head bent and she cried deep sobs of anguish. After several moments she mumbled, "Enough." She wiped her tears and went to work on heating up water in the kettle. She stirred the embers until a nice flame rose. She made quick work of changing from Lachlan's borrowed clothes to her own chemise and gown. Then she stood fidgeting and gnawing on her lower lip until the water heated to a soothing warmth. After pouring it into a chipped basin, she entered the bedchamber to find Sebastian watching her intently. At least watching her with one open eye. The eye that had been swollen shut by the highwaymen, and finally opened the previous day, was closed again, thanks to her brother.

"If ye keep getting injured, ah will be out of clothes." Heat infused her cheeks at the implication of her words. "I dinnae mean..."

"I understand."

She turned her back, lifted her skirts, and tore a strip off her chemise. Dipping the cloth into the basin, she wrung out the excess water and gently bathed the blood off his face and neck. "Ah can't believe Ian did this tae ye. Ah'm sorry. My brother is verra much like Paw."

"I'm glad it was me he took his anger out on instead of you."

His words had her insides fluttering.

"Thank ye. But ah would have preferred he took his anger out on someone other than ye."

Sebastian hissed when she came across a nasty gash on his forehead.

"Sorry."

"No need. I'm sorry you have to keep taking care of me."

Her fingers vibrated as she unbuttoned and removed the shirt Lachlan had lent Sebastian, then gasped at the colorful bruises covering his chest. "Dear God, my brother is a monster. Does it hurt?"

Sebastian laughed, then sucked in his breath. "Hurts. Probably broke a few ribs."

"Ah need tae get more cloth and wrap them up tightly. The more ye move the more they'll hurt. Best tae keep ye immobile for a spell."

"In case you haven't noticed, I'm not very mobile anyway."

"Yes, weel," she stuttered. "Ah'm sorry."

"Stop apologizing," he snapped. "Sorry. If it were not for you and Lachlan, I'd be dead. So I'm glad I'm alive. Recent beating notwithstanding."

"Ye are a good mon, Sebastian Seabrook. Ah can't understand why Marissa ran off and married someone else. Surely she must be daft."

He chuckled, which turned into coughing fits. "Ouch. Don't make me laugh. Not that Marissa running off to Gretna

Green is a laughing matter. But truthfully, her captain is a good man. Marissa will be happy with him. Something I'm not sure she would have be with...Never mind. He inhaled and his body tensed when she ran the warm cloth across his chest and stomach.

"So..."

"Don't say the word," he hissed. "You have no idea how sorry I am that you feel the need to be sorry for something you had no control over."

"No control," she cried as she continued to bathe his chest. Try as she might she couldn't help but stare at his hard muscles. Her eyes kept drifting to the line of dark blonde hair trailing down into his breeches. She'd seen his manhood. Felt it when they toppled onto the bed several days ago. Her mother didn't raise her to be wonton, but at this moment she'd have given anything to reach beneath the waistband and curl her hand around his member.

"Teagan," Sebastian said in a concerned voice. "If this is too much for you, Lachlan can help me. Bloody hell, he should be the one to do this anyway. An innocent shouldn't be exposed to a man's nakedness."

"My mother trained me tae heal. There is nothing ah havenae seen that would make me lose my senses."

"If you say so."

By the way he spoke she knew she didn't fool him. His nakedness did move her, and by the thoughts entering her mind, Lachlan should be the one cleaning up his cuts and bruises. Because if she kept this up she was liable to do some-thing scandalous. Like place her lips on his bruises to soothe away his pain. Or swipe her tongue across his cuts in hopes of helping them heal.

❄

HAVING Teagan's gentle and loving hands on his exposed skin was tortuous. When she first stepped into the cottage and looked over his battered body then locked her emerald green eyes on him, all air had escaped his lungs. The compassion, anger, and guilt shining in the depths of her eyes was like a punch to the gut. And he knew how that felt as he'd been repeatedly punched during the past day.

This punch to the gut was much worse because he was the cause of her pain and anguish. Hadn't she been through enough in her short life? At her young age she should be attending soirées and balls with nothing more pressing on her mind than what gown to wear or whose name was on her dance card. What eligible gentleman caught her eye and would he visit the next day for tea. She should not be running for her life from her father of all people. Nor betrothed to a monster.

Even with only one useful eye, he could read her emotions. Just now as she bathed his chest, her eyes dropped to his breeches and her cheeks flamed a becoming shade of pink. She may be innocent, but she was curious. The more she looked, the harder his cock became. She would be blind not to see the bulge protruding in his breeches.

Easy, Sebastian. Your body has been pummeled again and again. You should not be having indecent thoughts about Teagan. Not now. Not ever. She needs your help not a seduction.

"What is happening outside?" He needed to redirect his thoughts.

"I havenae a clue. Excuse me while ah find out."

"Steady," Sebastian told himself. Deep breaths hurt like a bugger. Light breaths not much different. Sebastian didn't know what he'd done to deserve these beatings, but he promised to be a better man. He would try not to think about Teagan and her full, kissable lips, her small, but womanly curves and her eyes that told the world her every thought.

"Lachlan will be in soon. The town's mon are escorting Ian and his mon tae the border with a message for Paw."

"Won't they just come back for you both?"

"Aye, probably. We have tae leave. Lachlan has managed tae procure two horses and a carriage. Ah know it willnae be easy traveling in yer condition, but we cannae leave ye behind."

Sebastian snorted. "No, I don't suppose you can. And I don't relish another beating by your brother. But do you think it wise for me to travel with my injuries?"

Emotions, once again, flashed in her eyes. Worry and guilt.

"What choice do we have? Teagan cast her eyes down at the ground, then looked at him as she took the few steps to his bedside. "Ah will do everything in my power tae keep yer body safe and give it the chance tae heal properly." Her hand reached out and pushed his hair off his forehead, and Sebastian could hardly breathe as she bent down and placed her warm, soft lips to his forehead. "Ah promise tae take care of ye while Lachlan drives the coach. Our transportation willnae be in the style and comfort ye'r used tae, but we will make do."

"Teagan," he breathed out as she lightly pressed her lips to his bruised cheek making him afraid to move and break this incredible closeness. It was as though she put him under some spell.

When her lips caressed his, he groaned and reached up with his good hand, cupped the back of her neck and pulled her in so he could taste her. To his delight, she didn't pull away but partook in the best kiss of his life. He devoured her. His tongue tangled with hers. And he almost lost it when she made little breathy sounds. That and she spread her scorching hot hands on his shoulders inflaming him more.

"Teagan," he said as he broke the kiss and began trailing kisses down her neck. "What you do to me. We must stop."

"Aye, ye must," Lachlan demanded.

Teagan jumped back and covered her mouth with her hand and blushed profusely.

Sebastian knew what she was going to say so he said it instead. "Sorry."

"Sorry?" she mouthed.

"Not really," he mouthed back so Lachlan could not hear.

His words had her smiling back shyly.

Teagan might not want his apology, but he was quite sure Lachlan did. "I'm sorry Lachlan. I took advantage of your sister. Please forgive me."

Laughter cut through the tension in the small room. "Ye are bedridden, ah highly doubt ye took advantage of my sister. Besides, if ye did she would have slapped ye. Time for this conversation another time. George, the blacksmith ah work for should be here any moment with the carriage and provisions. 'Tis high time we took ye back tae yer family. Then Teagan and ah will travel tae London and ask the prince for an audience."

"My brother will get you an audience with the prince. Do not worry."

"Thank ye. Ah hear horses, George must have arrived. Teagan, please go make the coach comfortable for Sebastian while ah help him make himself presentable. Cannae take him out half-naked now, can we?"

Once Teagan was out of the cottage, Lachlan helped him put on a clean shirt. "Tread kindly where my sister's heart is concerned. She has a big one, and I'd hate tae have tae call ye out at dawn for breaking it."

"This is not the proper time, but when everything is settled, could I court her, with your permission?"

Lachlan chuckled. "Aye, ye have my permission and my blessing, but dinnae need it. In case ye havenae noticed, my sister has a mind and will of her own and damn any mon getting in the way of something or someone she wants."

Sebastian had seen just how strong-minded she was. Somehow that made her even more appealing to him. Life with her would never be dull. What was he saying? He wanted to court her, not spend the rest of his life with her? Or did he?

CHAPTER EIGHT

EMMA, BELLA, AND AMELIA SAT IN THE DRAWING ROOM, each working on an embroidery piece for Emma's baby when the butler entered and announced a missive had just arrived.

"Thank you," said Emma as she took the sealed letter addressed to her husband. Under normal circumstances she would have left it on his desk in his study, but with him gone and no telling when he would return, she opened it. "Who can this be from?" Her eyes scanned the parchment, and she felt all the color drain from her face.

"Oh dear. Sebastian got lost during a terrible storm and was thrown from his mount and hurt."

"What?" Both Amelia and Bella cried at once.

"He states he is recovering with a brother and sister near Northumberland and that he suffered a large, deep gash on his leg, a broken arm and a skull fracture. He may not be able to travel for a fortnight or more." She scanned the letter then continued. "He apologizes to Wentworth for not being able to make it to our half-sister and could he please dispatch Smythe for the quest. He says he will be home as soon as he's able."

"What! That's all. Please tell me he wrote more than that," Amelia said with worried eyes.

"Actually, Amelia, he didn't write this, it's in someone else's handwriting. A women's I would guess."

"What should we do?" Bella asked as she stood and began pacing the room. "We need to speak to Bridgeton and Myles. Are they home?"

"I believe I hear them now." Amelia hurried out of the room and came back moments later with the men.

"What is this I hear about Sebastian being injured?" Myles said as he kissed his wife's flushed cheeks.

Bella handed over the thin parchment and waited as both Myles and Bridgeton scanned the contents.

"It says he is recovering nicely. Should we worry?" Myles stated.

Emma honestly didn't know what to say. "I wish my husband were here."

Bridgeton and Myles looked at each other with concern. Which didn't make Emma's nerves settle down any. Not to mention the baby was moving around making her uncomfortable.

"I wish we were in London." Myles sent another silent look to Bridgeton. "It will be two or three days before we can expect to hear anything back from Smythe. I'll send word immediately. Until then there is nothing we can do. Bridgeton and I can't very well set off and leave you ladies alone. Wentworth would have our heads on spikes if we did."

"We can't have that," Bella said as she stood up and slid her hand into her husband's. "I am worried though."

"I admit I am too," Myles stated. "Not about Wentworth and Spencer but about Sebastian and the medical care he is receiving."

"Can't we all travel by coach to Northumberland and take him back home with us?" Bella asked.

"Bella," Amelia said with a frown. "Emma can't travel that extensively with a baby due soon."

"I know. I just can't stand here and do nothing."

AS DINNERTIME APPROACHED, Emma's nerves twitched below the surface of her skin. She didn't relish explaining to her mother-in-law what had happened to Sebastian. Thankfully, the dowager wasn't one to take to fits and needing smelling salts. She handled the news well.

"That went better than expected," Emma said as she, Bella, and Amelia retired to the drawing room to await Bridgeton and Myles as they shared brandy in Wentworth's study.

"Mother always takes news well at first." Amelia sat on the settee and smoothed her skirts. "By tomorrow she will be beside herself with worry and will keep to her rooms to pray.

"Indeed, she will," Emma interjected. "But she is the strongest woman I know. By day two she will be back to her normal self and insisting on helping with our charity. Do you suppose we should tell her about my gothic novels? It will give her something else to dwell on."

"Knowing my mother," Bella said, "she already suspects something."

Emma gasped. "What makes you think that?"

"Just a feeling. When she talks about the books by Anna Smith, she looks at you and smiles secretly. And her eyes tell the same thing. She knows. She is just waiting for you to tell her."

Emma sank down into the settee with a sigh. "Now I feel terrible keeping secrets from her."

"Nonsense." Bella smiled. "Mother loves games. When she's ready to reveal her knowledge of you as the author, you will be the first to know. Meanwhile, I wish the gentlemen would join us. I can't stand the waiting."

Just then two sets of footsteps entered the drawing room. "Did I hear someone mention gentlemen," Myles said as he made a beeline to the sideboard, poured brandy into two crystal glasses, and handed one to Bridgeton."

"Yes. I'm having a difficult time with all the waiting. Honestly, Myles..." Bella exhaled. "When will we hear something?"

"Truth?"

Bella glared at her husband. "Yes. The truth."

"My dear, we went over this earlier. It will be a sennight or longer before Smythe reaches Sebastian. And that's if he rides like the devil. May I suggest Emma start a new novel and have you and Amelia help. And don't try and tell me you have never given her suggestions about her stories."

"Yes, well, only when she asks," Bella said, looking guilty."

"I'm asking," Emma said. "I have a story in my head, but I'm having trouble penning it. Perhaps tomorrow afternoon when the children are having their naps, we can meet in my chambers and talk the storyline over. Per usual my hero and heroine are not behaving as I want them to. You would think since I married them last book, they would get along better? But no, she is too stubborn and he is too old fashioned."

"You lost me." Myles chuckled. "But I think it is a splendid idea."

Bella agreed, although Emma knew she would much rather be taking to the road in hopes of rescuing Sebastian.

CHAPTER NINE

Teagan's cheeks warmed as she daydreamed about Sebastian's surprisingly soft lips pressed against hers. When his tongue swept inside her mouth, she'd hesitated, not knowing people did such a thing. But then it seemed natural to join hers with his. Natural and a little on the wanton side. Now that she'd experienced a real kiss for the first time, she wanted more. But only with Sebastian. She wanted to run her hands across his naked chest again and dip her tongue inside his mouth and hear and feel the moan rise up his throat. Her hands flew to her cheeks. "Stop these improper thoughts," she said to herself.

"Is everything ready? Ah dinnae think we should waste another second. Who knows if Ian will go tae Paw first or pursue us?"

Shaking her head to remove her scandalous thoughts, she continued to make a nice soft pallet for Sebastian on one of the narrow benches in the carriage with all the blankets she could find in the cottage. They may be moth eaten and a little threadbare, but they were clean. She'd washed them herself when they'd first arrived. He could sit against the sidewall with his legs spread out on the bench. Not the most comfortable position for someone as tall as Sebastian, but it would be best for his still healing leg, his arm, and now his broken and bruised ribs. She did worry overmuch for his leg. It may not have been broken, but the gash had been deep to the bone. Who knew if there was any permanent damage to muscle or tendon?

Worry etched in her mind about its healing. She prayed the beating by Ian and the long carriage ride wouldn't leave him crippled. But what other option did they have? None, thanks to her brother who she had no doubt would backtrack from the border and seek their whereabouts, making this trip all the more dangerous for Sebastian's healing. They had to make haste and keep to lightly traveled roads, putting them in more danger from highwaymen. Not to mention Lachlan didn't know the roads to begin with.

"Aye. Ah'll be right in tae help with Sebastian," Teagan said."

"No need, ah'll go get him," Lachlan replied."

"Before ye do, ye need tae ken something Ian said. Do ye remember the rumors amongst the servants about Maw being pregnant when she wed Paw?"

Lachlan shrugged his shoulders. "Ah never gave it a thought. Dinnae matter as long as they were wed before we were born, so we were nae bastards. But right now we have other things tae worry about. We can sort out the rest when we are safe."

"But there is more, much more Ian confessed to me."

"It needs tae wait until we are safe," Ian said as he walked away and entered the cottage.

Teagan wanted to scream after her brother, but he was right. This conversation could wait. Finding safety could not.

Next thing she knew Lachlan and Sebastian came into

view. Sebastian leaned heavily on Lachlan. "Can ye get the crutch ah made from the bedroom?"

"Aye." Teagan was happy to have something to do besides stand and watch Sebastian struggle to not show any pain as he made his way to the carriage.

Minutes later they were underway. Lachlan drove the coach while Teagan sat on the bench opposite Sebastian's. "How is yer leg and yer ribs? Do ye need me tae adjust the blankets for ye?"

"I'm fine, Teagan. Don't fuss over me. My brother's friend and mine as well, Amesbury, was in a tragic carriage accident which took the lives of his parents and sister…"

"Oh, how terribly sad," she interrupted."

"Yes, it was. Amesbury broke his back and the doctors said he would never walk again. Well, that didn't go over well with him. Months later he began walking with a cane, determined to go on living for his family members who couldn't. Now years later, no one would know what he went through. Only late at night or in the privacy of his home does he use his cane. When out in polite society, he pretends to feel no pain and fights to hide his limp. If he can recover, then so can I. I will not let my injuries keep me from dancing at the next ball, or riding, or going on hunting parties."

"Ah am sorry for yer friend," Teagan said with a heavy heart. She didn't want to ever imagine life without her brother. "Yer friend may have healed physically, but what about from the loss of his loved ones?"

Sebastian cleared his throat. "Yes, well, that's another story altogether."

"Are ye allowed tae share it?"

She knew by the way his brows furrowed he was contemplating the reasoning behind her question.

"I don't know. Nobody but those inside our close circle of family and friends knows about his struggles."

"Ah understand. But if ye told me, ah wouldnae tell a soul."

"As long as it goes no further than you and me. The doctors gave him laudanum for the pain. They said he would need the drug for the rest of his life. Amesbury became addicted to it in a bad way. Wentworth and our other friend, Myles, think Amesbury was trying to die."

"Oh dear."

"Then one night he almost succeeded...to die, that is. Since then he has recovered and put the anguish and loss of his family behind him. I'm quite convinced he still deals with terrible pain and sadness on a daily basis, but he no longer takes laudanum."

"How terribly sad for him. Ah hope tae meet yer family and friends ye speak so highly of someday."

"Oh, you will when we arrive at Stony Cross Manor."

Now it was her turn to worry. Worry about their safety on making Stony Cross Manor without Ian overtaking and killing them. But she didn't need to bring it up. Sebastian knew this, and yet he was willing to travel with them and put his life in danger once again.

"I know what you're thinking?" he said with a somber expression.

"Ye most certainly do not." She couldn't very well admit that he knew her so well.

"You are worried about my safety. Well, I'm worried about yours. That brother of yours is a monster. His eyes, when he would question me or hit me, were blacker than black and void of any emotions except rage. I'm finding it difficult to believe he is your brother?"

"Half-brother."

"Half..."

"Aye. Ian told me back at the cottage and ah'm inclined to believe him. But please keep it to yourself as ah havenae told

Lachlan yet. We'd both heard Maw was with child with me and Lachlan when she wed my paw. But we had no idea he wasnae our real Pa. It does explains why Paw hates us so and wants Ian tae inherit the title and lands. Lachlan is not his offspring by blood, only in name and because the duke signed the birth registry as our paw. In our society, that makes Lachlan the true heir."

"So that is why he is adamant in killing Lachlan. But why you?"

"Unfortunately, while Maw lived Paw tolerated our presence. He dinnae go out of his way tae be kind, he just didnae bother with us at all. Which was perfect for Lachlan and myself. Because when Paw did go on a rage, we would hide."

Anyway, my maw took ill and passed. The night we put her in the ground, he shot Lachlan, imprisoned him in the dudgeon to die, and gave me tae that beast of a mon. But Lachlan already explained all this to ye." Teagan swallowed the bile rising up her throat at the memory of that horrible night.

"Thank God, you are a strong willed and resourceful woman. And that Lachlan had a loyal valet. What do you suppose your father has done to him for his help in aiding his escape?"

"Oh dear, I hadnae thought about his safety. If Paw kens he helped Lachlan, he will be killed or worse. Imprisoned in the dungeon tae die a slow and tortuous death from starvation and the elements. He will freeze tae death during the winter without blankets." Teagan sat up straight on the bench and took a deep breath. "When we stop for the night, ah'll inquire as tae his safety. But if ah ken my brother at all, his valet was weel taken care of. May we change the subject? All this talk about death and danger is making me anxious."

❄

TEAGAN WASN'T the only one anxious. Lachlan sat holding the reins, driving the coach. Something he'd never done in his entire life. George had given him quick instructions, and he seemed to be doing well enough. The horses were used to pulling a carriage, which was fortunate for them all. Lachlan just hoped their luck stayed with them for the entire journey.

Bad weather, highwaymen, or his brother could cause a disaster. Meanwhile he stayed to the rough road George told him about and in several hours' time they should arrive at an Inn where the horses could be fed and rested, and they could have a hot meal and comfortable lodgings for the night.

While they traveled over bumps, rocks, and holes in the road he wondered how Sebastian was doing. He imagined his ribs were screaming out every time the carriage dipped and jarred. Not to mention his leg and arm. Hopefully this trip would not set the man back on his healing.

Something else weighed heavy on his mind. What exactly had Ian said to his sister? Lachlan had his suspicions over the years as to his parentage. But to his knowledge Teagan never had, besides thinking Mother and Father had made love at least once before speaking their vows, hence why they were hurried. Did Ian know the whole truth? The one Lachlan had guessed at shortly after their mother took sick? That their father was not really their father?

ON THE SECOND day of travel, the heavens opened up and damn if the coach didn't leak right onto Teagan's bench. Sebastian groaned with frustration at not being able to relieve Lachlan at the reins. He, no doubt, was soaked down to his skin and chilled to the bone. The weather had taken a drastic turn, bringing cold air. The last thing they needed was

Lachlan getting sick. The man had been through enough already.

Sebastian thought it foolish to use up most of the blankets making a soft pallet for his broken body. "Teagan, please help me remove these blankets from beneath me. I'm perfectly capable of sitting on the sparsely cushioned bench. And for God's sakes, come and share my seat. I won't have you catching a cold or worse, pneumonia on my behalf. That leak will drench the cushion and thus eventually, your clothing. Please."

He knew his words were harsh, but he felt like lashing out at something. Someone. Too bad that someone was the beautiful lady sharing this carriage and trying to save all their lives. She deserved much better than his behavior. And by the look she gave him, she didn't appreciate his words or tone either.

"I'm sorry. I shouldn't take my frustrations out on you. You and Lachlan are trying to help me while dealing with your own dire situation."

She jutted her chin up and damn, she looked determined and cute at the same time, making his insides stir with awareness.

After what seemed like forever, she finally moved from her seat. Gently, with his help, they removed all the blankets from beneath him. Carefully she adjusted his leg across the narrow aisle, and propped it up on the opposite bench far from the leak.

Teagan hesitantly sat beside him and covered them up with several blankets to ward off the chill. Without thinking, Sebastian wrapped his good arm around her back and pulled her close so they could share body heat.

"Sebastian...Lord Sebastian. Ah think we should address each other properly because we will arrive at yer family's estate soon, and ah don't want tae ostracize myself with bad etiquette."

"If you wish, Lady Teagan. Whatever you ask of me I will do."

The feel of her chest rising and falling soothed him. Her head tucked beneath his chin had the tantalizing scent from her hair drifting to his nostrils, causing them to flare. *Easy Sebastian. She's been in your arms for seconds, and you're already thinking improper thoughts.* Not to mention the stirrings in his pants.

"Tell me about your mother?"

Her body tensed and he thought she'd ignore his query, but then her body settled deeper within his. "She was beautiful and strong. She ran the house. Including keeping my paw in line. He was a poor, homeless duke when he married Maw. His castle had been ruined in the border wars with England. It was her dowry that rebuilt Murray Castle and kept them in the lifestyle befitting a family of a duke."

"Hmm, she had one large dowry."

"Aye, it must have been. She taught me how tae take care of the sick as her maw taught her. It is a tradition among the women in my family. He fought her everyday on it. Saying nay duchess of his would spoil her hands with tending tae servants or tenant farmers."

"Must have angered him to not get his way."

The sound of Teagan's laughter had him joining in with her.

"That is an understatement. He hated it. Hated her and me for nae being able tae control us. Yet he feared her, her paw, and brothers. They'd threatened him many times that they would nae hesitate tae cast him off his lands if he didnae treat her as due her station as a duchess. My grandpaw might nae have been a titled man, but a richer gentry ye would nae find in all of Scotland."

"Why did you not seek his help?"

Tension rolled through her body and he hugged her closer

to his side, ignoring the twinging pain in his ribs. The pain was nothing if he could comfort her and keep her warm.

"That is how we ken our paw was truly evil. Right after my maw died, he sent men tae my grandpaw's estate, killed him then went on tae my uncles' homes and had them killed tae."

He didn't have to hear her crying to know she was. She'd become quiet, and her body trembled ever so slightly. "Teagan, I'm sorry. What kind of monster kills another person? Why did you not go to the authorities? Certainly..."

"We didnae trust the local authorities. They might have been under Paw's rule. And we only ken about the deaths because Paw taunted them in Lachlan's face right before he locked him in the dungeon. Ah dinnae find out until we escaped. Ah think Lachlan would have kept it from me if he could. But ah kept insisting we travel tae them. Finally he broke down and told me the truth. So many loved ones dead by my evil paw's hands."

She pulled away from Sebastian and looked him in the eye. The contradiction between the silent tears staining her cheeks to the determination in her eyes was startling.

"Nay, not my real paw. No doubt he had him killed as weel."

"Oh, Teagan." Sebastian's heart ached for her. Such tragedy for one family to behold. He reached out with his good hand and used his thumb to wipe the tears from her face, then he rested his palm on her cheek for silent support. Her hand came up and covered his, holding it to her face.

"Thank ye. Ah realize tragedy strikes families every day, but when 'tis yers 'tis different. Somedays ah'm paralyzed with grief and then fear. Fear that Lachlan will be next, and ah will truly be alone for the rest of my life."

Sebastian turned to face her on the bench. Ignoring the

screaming burn in his ribs and thigh was easy once he looked into her eyes and was lost in the green depths full of turmoil.

Even though their conversation was deeply sad and moving, he couldn't help himself for what he did next. It seemed only natural. Everything about Teagan since he awoke from his attack to find starling emerald eyes assessing his injuries had seemed like fate. And he'd fallen into her spell...hard.

The first time they kissed came to him in his dreams at night. He lowered his head and pressed his lips to hers, which were moist and salty from her tears. He pulled back and whispered, "Teagan?" When nothing but a sigh escaped her lips he crushed her to him and took what they both wanted.

In the back of his mind he told himself to be gentle and take it slow. The only time she'd been this close to a man was the night she'd been attacked by the monster her not-real father betrothed her to. But then she wrapped her arms around his neck and pulled him closer and proceeded to take as much as he gave.

He was lost to everything surrounding them. The constant drip, drip of the leaking roof. The sound of the horse's hooves digging into the mud and Lachlan's voice encouraging them on. The wind whistling and the rocking of the carriage. Even the pain from his injured body. All was forgotten save for the woman whose lips pressed against his.

Taking it deeper, he thrust his tongue inside and tasted every crevice of her mouth. Never to have enough and wanting more than he could ever have. He gasped, pulled back, and cradled her face in his hands and smiled while ignoring the pounding of his heart and the throbbing in his breeches. "Thank you."

"For what? "She smiled back with kiss swollen lips, and he groaned knowing he was responsible.

"For risking ruin by letting me kiss you. For saving my life from the highwaymen even though at first you wanted to leave me for dead." He had to lighten the mood, or he was liable to lift her skirts and take her innocence on the road in the worn and leaking carriage.

"Aye, indeed. Ah did want tae leave ye. Ah thought ye already dead and possibly one of Paw's men. After we dragged yer beaten body back home and ye opened yer good eye for the first time, ah lost myself into the deep blue depths of it."

So much for lightening the mood. She brought it right back to sensual. "Teagan."

"Kiss me Sebastian. Ah want tae forget what's happening around us and get lost in yer kisses."

Who was he to disappoint a lady? The moment their lips touched, he knew he'd never be the same gentleman he'd been when he left his family home in search of his half-sister. His heart belonged to another for the first time in his life. It made him understand why people risked everything for love.

CHAPTER TEN

Safe, cherished. Those were the words that came to Teagan's mind when she looked at Sebastian's handsome face right before he dipped his head and kissed her only minutes ago. The first time he kissed her back at the cottage was a first for her, and she'd been hesitant and afraid she'd do something wrong.

The second kiss seemed as though Sebastian couldn't get enough of her. Like he wanted to drink her in and never go thirsty.

This kiss, the third, was gentle, loving, and her whole body trembled with need. A need she didn't understand. Her belly fluttered, and she felt the overwhelming need to close her legs or touch herself down there. Is this what love felt like? Or was she developing loose morals?

"Sebastian," she breathed when he pressed feather light kisses down her neck and across to her opposite ear.

"Yes, sweetheart?" he said as he sucked on her earlobe, causing her whole body to tingle.

"Ye shouldnae."

He chuckled, then lightly bit her lobe. "I shouldn't?"

"Sebastian," she moaned as his hand slipped inside her pelisse and cupped her breast. Her day dress and chemise were so threadbare it was as though he touched bare skin. The sensation of him caressing her had her wiggling on the seat and feeling those feeling down low intensify.

For some reason he removed his hand. Just as she leaned forward, hoping to connect with his hand again, she realized what Sebastian already knew. They had come to a stop and she heard voices.

"Hand me the crutch and stay here regardless of what you hear."

"Ye cannae be serious. Ye'll break yer neck getting out of this carriage." Fear for all their safety had her insides vibrating and her voice along with it.

Before either one of them could exit the coach, the door opened to a very wet and shivering Lachlan. But fortunately for all, the rain had stopped.

"These mon here say they ken ye and were sent by yer brothers-in-law."

With the help of Lachlan, Sebastian was able to quit the carriage and lean on his crutch to greet the three strangers. "Smythe," Sebastian said with a wide grin when he finally recognized the man beneath the sopping wet hat. "You have no idea how glad I am to see you."

The one she presumed was named Smythe answered. "Likewise. Northborough and Bridgeton were beside themselves after they received your missive."

"What about Wentworth?"

"He had already gone out looking for you with Mr. Spencer. They traveled to Carlisle thinking you were lost along the way. Your brother had a strange feeling you were in trouble. After receiving word from Bridgeton and Northborough, I agreed."

"Yes, indeed. If it weren't for Lord Lachlan and Lady Teagan I would be dead."

Smythe acknowledged each of them with a nod of his head. "The Seabrook family is forever in your debt. Please, may we escort you to Stony Cross Manor?"

"They winnae be indebted tae us when they find out the whole truth," Lachlan muttered, and Teagan hoped nobody else heard but her.

"Thank you," Sebastian said, giving her brother a wide-eyed look.

Yes indeed, Teagan mused. Others had heard.

"Would one of your men be so kind as to give Lord Lachlan a break from the reins?" Sebastian added.

"Be glad to drive the coach myself," Smythe answered as he tied his horse's reins to one of his men's saddles.

This time when the wheels began turning, Teagan sat beside her brother on a pile of blankets to keep them dry from the wet cushions. Sebastian relaxed once again with his leg up on the bench. And for the first time since they set out from Murray Castle, Teagan had hope for the future and for their safety.

THREE DAYS hence and no trouble from her brother. Teagan looked out the coach window at Stony Cross Manor. The name fit. It was large and made mostly of grey stone. Once the carriage came to a stop, voices could be heard outside. Voices she presumed belonged to Sebastian's family.

The door burst open, the stairs put in place, and Teagan found herself being handed to a handsome gentleman with dark hair touched with grey and warm eyes.

"Welcome. I'm Bridgeton. We'll make formal introductions when you've gotten settled and cleaned up."

"Thank ye," she mumbled as she landed on wobbly legs after having spent so much time in a moving coach. Before she could greet the rest, she was whisked away by an older, plump woman who introduced herself as the housekeeper.

"I'll get you settled into your room and leave you in the capable hands of Gretchen, Lady Amelia's maid. Water is being heated for your bath, which will be ready momentarily. Welcome to Stony Cross Manor, milady."

After the housekeeper left with a curtsy, Teagan spun around and took in the opulent room decorated in subtle shades of green and cream. A large mahogany four poster bed sat in the middle of the room with two small chests of drawers on either side. The cream comforter and numerous green and cream pillows beckoned her. One glance at her filthy clothing, and she took a seat on a wooden chair at the small dressing table and waited.

She didn't wait long as a knock sounded on the door, and it was opened by a young woman in her late teens.

"Milady, I'm Gretchen and I'll be attending you today. Your bath should be...ah, it is here already."

Two servants came in with a large metal tub while two more filled it with buckets of steaming water. Teagan tried not to drool. When was the last time she'd had a decent bath? Not since she escaped from her home.

After the male servants left, Gretchen helped her undress and assisted her into the decadently warm water.

"Hmmm. This is heaven. As long as ah can reach the soap and washcloth, ah can bathe myself."

"Yes. Milady. I'll be fetching you some clean clothing."

Bathing alone in a bedchamber that didn't belong to her, in the house of a duke she'd yet to meet, should have made her nervous, and yet for some reason she felt completely and utterly relaxed. Picking up the soap and cloth left on a stool next to the tub, she inhaled the lavender fragrance and smiled. "Perfect," she said to herself as she bathed and washed and rinsed her hair.

When still the maid didn't return, she leaned back and closed her eyes. Every muscle in her body relaxed as she let the warm water transform her from dirty and travel worn to clean and smelling like her favorite wildflowers.

When Gretchen came back, she helped Teagan dress in a high-waist beautiful light blue linen day dress with a scooped neckline and deeper blue ribbon accents. She wondered who the dress and undergarments belonged to, and she imagined she would meet the lady soon enough.

One of Sebastian's sisters no doubt. Or possibly the duke's wife? Whoever the clothing belonged to, she was close in size to herself as the dress fit almost perfectly.

When the maid left, Teagan didn't know what to do. Did she leave her chamber and seek out people or stay and wait to be called upon. She didn't have long to find out as mere minutes after Gretchen left a knock sounded on the door.

"Please come in."

Teagan eyed the door with excitement, wondering who would enter, and she smiled when three beautiful women stepped inside the room. One of them was a lovely pregnant lady with light hair, blue eyes, and fair skin. The other two looked like sisters, only one was fair and one dark. One had Sebastian's coloring and eyes.

"Hello," Teagan said, wondering who would speak first.

"Hello, welcome to our home," said the pregnant lady with a lovely American accent. "I'm Emma, the Duchess of Wentworth, and these are Sebastian's sisters. Amelia, the Countess of Bridgeton and Bella, the Countess of North-borough."

Teagan curtsied. "Hello. Ah'm Lady Teagan Murray."

"Yes. We know," said the Countess of Northborough. "Please call me Bella. When it is just family here, we are a little lapse in formality. Although I would call my brother Wentworth or duke. He can be stuffy at times."

"No, he is not." Emma laughed. "It's your mother who wants us to be formal at all times."

"Please don't mind them," the one named Amelia interjected. The one married to the handsome gentleman who assisted her from the carriage earlier. "It's been a while since we had a new female in the house to gossip with."

"Gossip? But ah dinnae ken anyone in England tae gossip about," Teagan said, liking these three women already. They seemed warm and friendly, and they appeared to care deeply about one another.

"That's fine," Bella said with a wave of her hand. "The three of us talk quite a lot. You can listen if you want."

"But first," Emma said. "It is teatime and everyone is awaiting us in the drawing room."

Teagan hesitated and swallowed. "Everyone?"

Bella linked her arm through Teagan's elbow and walked toward the door, pulling her along. "Don't worry, our family is friendly. Everyone is welcome. Especially a brother and sister who saved our brother, Sebastian's, life. I can't wait to hear the details of the story. Sebastian didn't have much to say about it."

"There isnae much tae tell."

"Liar," Bella whispered close to her ear. "Here we are."

Teagan found herself whisked inside a blue drawing room, settled on a soft midnight blue velvet settee in between Bella and Amelia. Facing her on matching upholstered chairs was Emma and who she presumed was the Dowager Duchess of Wentworth.

One glance across the room and she eyed three men sitting and having a serious conversation. At least by their expressions she thought serious. One she knew as Bridgeton, the other must be Northborough, and her heart pounded when she saw Sebastian resting in a chair with his leg up on a footstool. He'd bathed and dressed in casual clothing. He turned her way and his somber expression was replaced with a breathtaking smile as he nodded his head in greeting, causing her heart to melt at his handsomeness, regardless of his bruised face and still swollen eye.

"My dear, Lady Teagan," the dowager began. "I am so very happy to make your acquaintance. And indebted to you and your brother for saving my son. It would have been a terribly tragedy if he'd been taken from us."

Teagan's cheeks heated with embarrassment at being praised by Sebastian's mother. "Ye are welcome. Has my brother been down? Ah havenae seen him since we arrived."

"I believe he has just entered." The dowager nodded in the direction of the double doors.

Lachlan paused to acknowledge the ladies whom she learned he'd met earlier. He kissed her cheek and whispered, "Ah like these people and ye look lovely." Then he crossed the room to join the men in conversation.

Teagan would love to know what they discussed. If she didn't know better, she would think they were planning something nefarious.

WHEN TEAGAN ENTERED the drawing room with his sisters, Sebastian's ears shut off the conversation Bridgeton and Myles were having, as important as it was, and focused his whole being on her. Dressed in finery, she was even more breathtaking than ever. Although she didn't need expensive clothing and accessories to be beautiful to him. Everything about her moved him. Dressed in rags, a chemise, or a ball gown and his feelings towards her would not change. To his mind and eyes no one could be more precious, elegant, or gorgeous than she.

"Sebastian," Bridgeton said with frown. "Are you listening? This is important. I would think you would want revenge against Ian Murray."

SOMETIME DURING HER first night at Stony Cross Manor Teagan got tired of staring at the ceiling, waiting to fall asleep. She donned a robe and wrapped a shawl around her shoulders. After lighting an oil lamp, she quietly strolled down the corridor, down the grand staircase, and into the drawing room they'd taken tea in that afternoon. If only she knew where the library was. A book would certainly help her fall asleep.

As she approached the open doors, a soft glow illuminating from the fireplace pulled her toward it. She placed her lantern on the mantel. The trip from her room through the chilly hallways had her shivering, and she pulled her shawl tight around herself and sighed. "There's nothing like a warm fire."

"I agree."

Startled, she spun around with one hand going to her throat as her heart exploded inside her chest. When her eyes connected with the gentleman sitting in a chair with his leg propped up on a stool, her heart didn't actually slowdown as one would think. It continued to pound, only this time it wasn't out of shock at finding she was not along. It was because Sebastian was the other occupant of the room.

"Ye startled me."

"My apologies. I figured it would be better to say something than have you confiding all your secrets to the flames, thinking you were alone.

"Ah would never do that?"

"Should you not be sleeping?" Sebastian said with a raised brow.

"Ah couldnae sleep."

"Me neither." He waved his hand to the empty chair beside his. "Please have a seat. You can still feel the heat from the fire here."

"Thank ye." She sat down and pulled her shawl together with trembling hands. "Have ye had word from yer brother?"

"No. But after resting tonight, Smythe and his men are going to travel to find him. Emma seems concerned."

"Perhaps she just misses him and wants him close by with her expecting and all."

Sebastian rubbed his hands in front of him. "It's bloody chilly tonight."

Teagan jumped up, went to the settee to retrieve a lap blanket, and covered Sebastian with it. She kept her eyes downcast, afraid if he saw her face he'd see the longing in her eyes. A longing for him she was still trying to sort out.

As she was just about to step away, he reached for her hand. "Do I make you nervous?"

"Sometimes." Was that her breathy voice?

"What's changed? I don't think I made you nervous before?"

Closing her eyes, she breathed in, hoping to steady herself. Her body trembled and her heart pounded as though it wanted to leap out of her chest. She'd never felt flustered like this before, and she didn't like it one bit.

"Everything is different now. Ye are nae bedridden. The stitches are ready tae be removed from yer leg and face. Yer arm and ribs must be feeling better and well on their way tae being mended."

Sebastian used his good leg to kick the footstool aside,

then he moved the lap blanket and tugged her hand so she fall into his lap with a gasp.

"Sebastian...yer leg."

"My leg is fine. The physician removed the stitches this afternoon. He said you did a good job. As good as he could have done. Now let yourself relax. I'll keep you warm. Besides, I've been dying to hold you again."

"So that is what is changed? Ah thought ye face seemed different. Before she realized it her fingers were tracing the thin red scar down one side of his face. "But what if someone sees us?"

"Sweetheart, the house is quiet. Everyone is asleep, and it will be two hours before the servants arise. So in the meantime it's just you and me."

"Ye and me," she murmured. He and I. It was scandalous and most improper for her to be in a room alone with him, never mind sitting on his lap dressed in her night rail. Once he pulled the lap blanket around them both and held her close, she didn't care who saw them. There was something undeniably comforting about Sebastian. She could no more stay away from him than a moth could stay away from a flame.

"Yer family is so nice. Ah'll admit Bella, Amelia, and Emma can be a bit much, but in a good and welcoming way. Ah never had a sister, but if ah did ah'd like tae think we'd be as close as they are."

Sebastian chuckled, causing his lap to shake. "Bella and Amelia have always been close. When Emma came to live with us, she fit right in. Two sisters became three."

"You told me before that Emma and Wentworth married. How long after they met did they wed?"

❄

SEBASTIAN SMILED THEN WINCED at the memory of when Emma first arrived, that and his ribs hurt. But the pain radiating from them would not interfere with the opportunity to hold Teagan close. This was the part of the story Sebastian didn't care to relate, but if he wanted a future with Teagan, and he did, he needed to be truthful from the start. "When Emma first came here, Wentworth and she appeared to dislike each other very much. Truth be told, I fell for Emma and asked her to marry me."

A little gasp was all he heard from Teagan, and he wondered what she was thinking. "She tried to turn me down, but I wouldn't listen and told her to think about it. Later that day, I came upon her and Wentworth in a compromising situation."

"Hate turned tae love?"

"Something like that. Anyway." He needed to get the words out before he changed his mind. "I attacked my brother."

Her gasp was quite a bit louder this time, but still she stayed silent. Still waiting, no doubt, for him to continue. "We fought. Emma stepped in between us. I was angry, I told him I was going to America to run Hamilton Oil for him. I left that afternoon and stayed at a hotel until I could purchase passage on a ship."

"Ah'm sorry. It must be hard on ye seeing Emma and yer brother together and so happy."

"Not anymore. I spent nearly two years in America, sold all Wentworth's holdings, and came home to realize I never really loved her at all. Oh, I love her like a sister, but nothing more."

"What is America like?"

Sebastian was so very thankful she didn't pursue his relationship or feelings for Emma. "I only traveled throughout Massachusetts. Boston is much like any bustling port and city in England. At times, if I closed my eyes and listened to the voices around me, I thought I was right here in England with all the British accents. There is still some unrest. The Indians pose a threat in the Midwest, but I never traveled there. While Myles was there he traveled all over. Met several Indians and said they are misunderstood. Also, I was told New Orleans is like a small France."

"Will ye go back someday?"

Will he? "Probably not. It was a nice adventure. I made Wentworth a lot of money in the sale of his holdings, and he transferred some of that wealth to me. So although I was born a second son, I am wealthy in my own right, thanks to Mr. Hamilton. Before Wentworth inherited, we worried he might be thrown in debtor's prison."

"Surely a duke wouldnae be subjected tae such a place?"

He liked that she took offence to his brother's plight. "We didn't believe it would come to fruition, but one never knew. Thank goodness my brother and Priney have such a good relationship."

"Speaking of the prince, when do ye think we can get an audience with him?"

"When my brother comes home, he'll send word. Are you still worried about your safety?" Sebastian hated that she had lived in such fear and didn't want her to ever feel that way again.

"Ah was never worried about mine, but Lachlan's. He needs tae die for Ian tae inherit, ah dinnae. My paw just hates me."

"I'm sorry. My father wasn't always a lying, cheating arse. But the last several years before he died, he took his anger out on those closest to him."

"What makes people do the things they do?"

He often asked himself the very same thing. "I wish I knew what made my father change. What made him drink himself to death? Spend the family fortune on mistresses and cards. Alas, it's something we will never know. I'm trying to resign myself to never knowing. I know it weighs heavily upon my brother. Probably more so as he was left with my father's messes to clean up. His debts, the estates falling into disrepair, and tenant farmers struggling to put food on their table."

"If you hadnae told me ah wouldnae have ken about the struggles."

"You might not have known, but the whole of the *ton* does. But I think I can speak for my family when I say we don't let the gossip bother us. Not anymore."

Teagan lay her head back against his chest, and he rested his cheek against her head. Everything about holding her felt right. Was this why he never married Marissa? Because he'd known, deep down, Teagan was out there waiting for him?

"Teagan." he nuzzled her hair. "I want to kiss you." His muscles coiled with need, his hands trembled with the urge to touch and feel her soft skin beneath his fingertips.

"Sebastian," she murmured as she looked up at him with desire and need in her eyes, making his heart soar.

He cradled her face in his hands and lowered his mouth to hers. Upon contact his body sizzled and he deepened the kiss. She moaned and curled her arms around his neck, pulling him even closer. The feel of her unbound breasts against his chest fueled his lust out of control. She made him feel out of control and on the verge of exploding. There was no way she couldn't feel his arousal pushing up against her behind.

Gasping for air, he pulled back and rested his forehead against hers. "Teagan. I want you. Do you understand what that means?" All air suspended from his lungs as he waited for her answer.

"Aye and nay."

He still couldn't breathe. "I won't compromise you, but I

need to touch you. Can I touch you?" More holding his breath for what seemed like an eternity. And then he heard the softest murmur.

"Aye."

"Oh, God, Teagan, I want you so much it's killing me." Besides a young widow he'd visited on occasion since his return from America, he'd been left to his own devices. He didn't believe in having a mistress, thanks to his father. So sex wasn't something Sebastian had on a regular basis, and his body was aroused beyond recent memory. He had to tamp it down and make this about Teagan. He didn't want to frighten her after her altercation with the brute she was affianced to. The same creature who tried to violate her. She needed to be handled gently and lovingly.

His lips trailed down the gentle curve of her neck, across the top of her bosom and up the other side. While his mouth cherished her, his good hand cupped her breast through the gossamer silk fabric and her nipples pebbled, begging for his attention.

Using his hand, he pulled her night rail down, exposing one small creamy breast. His mouth found her pert nipple, suckled and laved it with his tongue, and he nearly came in his breeches at the sensual noises coming through Teagan's open lush lips.

CHAPTER ELEVEN

TEAGAN COULD DO NOTHING BUT LET SEBASTIAN HAVE HIS way with her. Her body was soft and pliant, her skin tingled with awareness, and she wanted more than anything to have his hands down there. What gave her peace of mind and made her able to give herself up to the pleasure of his hands and mouth on her was that she trusted him not to take her virginity. And she knew, without a doubt, he would never be rough with her, never cause her pain.

When his hands cupped and kneaded her breasts, heat spread throughout her entire body. But that didn't compare to when he pulled her night rail down, exposing her bosom to the cool air only to be covered with his hot mouth. When his tongue laved her nipple and he took it between his teeth and gently bit her, she almost fell off his lap. His arms steadied her. So she did the only thing she could think of, she wiggled her bottom against his engorged manhood which had him groaning and rocking his hips up against her behind

"Teagan, you drive me to distraction. Can I touch you down there?" He moaned. "I promise your virginity will be intact."

Teagan didn't have to think. The words escaped her lips without a thought. "Aye. Oh, please, touch me." Who was this wanton woman begging to be touched? What had Sebastian done to her? If she didn't guard her heart, she'd think she already loved him...just a little.

His warm, rough hand caressed her ankle, slowly and torturously it traveled over her calf, paused at her knee then continued on up the inside of her thigh until his hand was there, but not there. It hovered just out of reach at the juncture of her thighs. Waiting and driving her crazy with need and curiosity. Just as she rose up her hips, his hand descended and cupped her and stilled. Her heart pounded so loudly it was all she could hear inside her head. Why didn't he move his hand? And then he did. One finger swirled around her, again and again ever so gently.

Never, ever, had she experienced such sensations bombarding her. Desire, fear, exhilaration, and need. Deep down a powerful need she didn't understand.

"Open for me, love?"

"Open?"

"Your legs," Sebastian said as he kissed her in a drugging kiss meant, no doubt, to tantalize her even more.

Sighing into his mouth, she relaxed her thighs open and his fingers were everywhere. Outside, inside, caressing her buttocks. *Oh my God* surely one died and went to hell after experiencing such naughty bliss.

Her stomach coiled up tight, her body pulsed down below. Yup, she was dying and she welcomed it.

"Sebastian, what is happening to me?"

She couldn't actually hear him smile, but she knew he was. She felt the tug of his lips against hers. "Relax and enjoy. You're experiencing your first sexual encounter and orgasm."

"Orgasm...ohhh...ohhh...dinnae...understand."

Stars burst before her eyes, and she gasped for air as her

body vibrated until finally she went limp. Sebastian pulled her night rail down and wrapped both arms around her waist and kissed her cheek. "You do now."

"What happened tae me?" she said breathlessly.

"Pleasure. I pleasured you. Damn, but you are one sensual woman. But I already suspected it the first time I kissed you."

"Do ah want tae be a sensual woman?"

Laughter bubbled out of Sebastian, and she couldn't help but join him. She didn't know why she laughed, she just felt happy and free and alive.

"With the right man, sensuality is nice. Very nice. I want to be the only man with the privilege of pleasuring you. The morning is coming fast. We must get you to your room before the servants rise."

Teagan looked around the room for his crutch and found only a cane and frowned. "Please be careful with the cane. It doesnae look sturdy enough for yer weight."

He snickered. "Yes, my dear nurse. I will be very careful. I can't wait to attend our first ball, so I can hold you close in a waltz."

She gasped and looked at him with a frown. "It will be sometime yet before ye take tae waltzing."

"I beg to differ." He nudged her off his lap and reached down for his cane, which had fallen onto the rug. "We must go."

As quietly as they could, they walked up the staircase and down the hallway to Teagan's bedchamber. Once outside the door, Sebastian pulled her into his arms and kissed her with so much emotion her knees nearly buckled.

Then he tucked a stray strand of hair behind her ear and walked away, limping on his cane. Her eyes were riveted and her feet refused to move as she watched him leave her hallway and enter another.

The soft creak of the door adjacent to hers had her jumping in her skin.

"So, that is the way of it with my brother," Bella said as she silently tiptoed toward her.

Heat scorched Teagan's cheeks and chest at being caught. "Ah..."

"I think it's wonderful. You two make a lovely couple. Does Lachlan know?"

"He has his suspicions."

"You are blushing and glowing." Bella smiled as she tiptoed back to her door and disappeared inside with a soft click.

Opening and closing the door without a noise was not easy, but Teagan believed she managed such a thing. Now she stood inside the room leaning against the door and hugging herself and reliving the intimate and sensual experience in Sebastian's arms. Should she worry that Bella knew? She didn't think so. She was married, she understood about the attraction between the opposite sexes. Besides, didn't she say, "They made a lovely couple?" Were they a couple? Would he approach Lachlan about courting her?

Somehow her feet moved toward her bed, she collapsed down, buried beneath the coverlet, and fell asleep with a smile on her face.

What seemed like a minute later, a knock sounded on her door and Gretchen came inside, opened the drapes, rummaged inside her wardrobe, and pulled out a pretty day dress in mint green.

"Where did all the clothes come from?" Because when Gretchen opened the wardrobe Teagan glimpsed numerous dresses and matching pelisses that were not there yesterday."

"Her Grace. She does not fit into them at the moment and was most gracious in offering them to you. Only little changes needed to be made."

Teagan didn't know what to say. The Seabrook family was so kind and generous to Lachlan and her, considering they were strangers.

"Would you like help dressing and styling your hair? It's such a lovely color it would be my honor to style it."

While Teagan had lived at Murray Castle, she'd had a ladies' maid, but Teagan preferred to do most everything by herself. Everything that is, except for tightening her stays, when she bothered to wear such confining clothing, and hair.

Gretchen seemed eager to help. "Aye, thank ye."

Half an hour later she found herself in the company of Bella, Amelia, and Emma as they made their way down to the breakfast room.

"So...you and Sebastian?" Emma said with a twinkle in her eyes.

"Emma," Bella scolded. "I told you not to say anything."

"Then I'll say it," Amelia interjected. "You and Sebastian. I think it's wonderful. I knew him and Marissa..."

"Amelia," Emma scolded.

"'Tis fine. Ah know about Marissa," Teagan said."

"He told you?" This from Bella.

"When he was unconscious after being attacked by the highwaymen he talked about Marissa. Ah asked him when he awoke. He told me everything." Teagan sighed. "How romantic, eloping with a man ye hardly know."

"Yes, well," Bella said. "Myles is not too pleased with the turn of events. But he would never keep Marissa from her happiness. I think he wants them to come home, so he knows they are both safe and he can finally give them his blessing. Not that the captain asked for it, but my husband will give it nonetheless."

"Ah hope tae get tae ken all three of yer husbands better. Northborough and Bridgeton seem...Ah'm afraid what ah have tae say may insult them, but they look in love. They look at ye, Bella and Amelia, with adoration and love. Ah hope someone looks at me that way."

Her three companions giggled. "Have you not seen Sebastian when he looks at you?" Bella asked. "I didn't have to catch you two in the hallway in the wee hours of the night enjoying each other's lips to know my brother had that look in his eyes yesterday during afternoon tea and again at dinner."

By the time they reached the sunny breakfast room, Teagan was warm and flustered. And it didn't help that Sebastian was the first person she rested her eyes on. Her cheeks inflamed even more, and she wondered what was happening to her. She'd never felt young and giddy, ever. Was she in love?

After fixing a plate with sausages, fruit, cheese, and coddled eggs, she sat down with a footman's assistance and was immediately brought warm chocolate.

"Good morning, Teagan, ah trust ye slept well?" Lachlan said to her with a knowing glint in his eyes. Did everyone know about Sebastian kissing her last night? Dear God, please don't let them know about what else he did to her. Even thinking about it now had her insides hot and bothered.

"Aye, dear brother, ah did. And ye?"

"Ah slept like the dead."

She didn't believe him. On close inspection, he looked rather tired. Dark circles encased his eyes and his face looked rather drawn. How much weight had he lost since their ordeal with their father? Strange, she didn't notice until now.

"Has there been any word from the duke?" Lachlan asked as he wiped his mouth with his cloth napkin.

"Not yet," Myles answered. "Smythe and his men left at first light. Hopefully they will be upon Wentworth and Spencer within several days. It may be a sennight or longer before we hear anything."

"I wonder if they have found Penelope yet," Emma said as

she looked over the rim of her cup. "With any luck they could already be traveling back."

"Let us hope so," The Dowager Duchess said.

CHAPTER TWELVE

AFTER DAYS OF TRAVEL, WENTWORTH AND SPENCER arrived at the small remote town outside of Carlisle and found lodgings at the Three Horses Inn. They sat in the private room for the gentry, eating rabbit stew and drinking a pint.

"While I went to the stables to see to the horses, did you inquire about Penelope?" Spencer asked over the top of his pint.

"Yes. The innkeeper and his wife have never heard of her. But she said they don't know many of the local townsfolk. They only began running the inn after her brother died several months ago."

"Too bad, it would've helped us in our search. I wish Penelope gave you an address instead of just the name of the bloody town."

"Yes, well, I wish she did too. But how hard can it be to find her. This town doesn't look all that big. First thing tomorrow we'll set out."

Bright and early after a quick breakfast of eggs and fresh rolls, Wentworth and Spencer set out looking for Penelope.

The first stop they made was to the local vicar. And it was a good thing they did because he had word of her. All the vicar could tell them was she had fled the home of the Viscount shortly after her mother had passed. She had been working as a scullery maid, and he didn't know why she didn't stay on.

Wentworth couldn't understand why she wouldn't stay in the employ of Viscount Hadley either. At least until she heard from him. Unfortunately, Wentworth didn't know Hadley or anything about the man. However, something deep inside his soul screamed that he wasn't a man to be trusted.

When he and Spencer arrived at the viscount's modest and nicely maintained estate, they were led immediately to the man's study where a rather large, balding middle aged viscount sat behind a large mahogany desk.

The viscount stood and gestured to two chairs facing the desk. "Welcome, Your Grace, Mr. Spencer. Please have a seat and tell me why you honor me with your presence today."

Wentworth sat and got right to the point of his visit. "I am inquiring as to the whereabouts of a young lady in your employ. A Miss Penelope Sullivan. Is she still with you?"

If Wentworth wasn't mistaken the viscount twitched.

"She was in my employ, a scullery maid, I believe. Her mother was my wife's ladies' maid. That was until she took ill and died recently. The day after I graciously paid to have a proper burial for her mother, the girl vanished."

"Does your wife know anything? Or the cook. Surely she confided in the cook as to her plans?"

"Possibly. I never inquired." The viscount rang the bell summoning a servant. "Please bring Mrs. Ellsworth to me."

They sat in silence until the cook arrived, looking over-worked and flustered. "Yes milord, how may I help you?"

The viscount explained the reason for Wentworth and Spencer's visit. Upon hearing the girl's name, the cook rung her hands together and looked even more disconcerted.

"I'm sorry, Your Grace, the miss left without a word to any of us in the kitchen. And honestly, she kept to herself. Only conversing with her mother. And nearing the end of her mothers' life, she spent all her spare time nursing her."

"Thank you, Mrs. Ellsworth. That will be all," the viscount said then focused on Wentworth. "I'm sorry we couldn't be of help to you in your search. If I may be so bold as to ask, why are you seeking the girl?"

"She is my half-sister." Without another word Wentworth and Spencer left. But Wentworth didn't miss the panicked look that crossed the viscount's features.

Once outside the home, Spencer addressed him. "He is hiding something."

"I agree." They walked their horses to the side of the estate where the servants' door was located and knocked. To Wentworth's surprise, the cook opened the door and hurried them inside the dark hallway.

"I knew you would come. So I waited, Your Grace." The cook glanced over her shoulder then began her story. "The viscount made subtle hints as to his interest in the girl. While her mother lived, he only cornered her and occasionally managed a groping. After her mother died," the cook crossed herself and muttered, "God rest her soul, she fled, afraid for her safety and virtue."

"Any idea where?"

"No, but she talked about a relative. You must be him."

Wentworth removed several coins from his pocket and placed them in the woman's work worn hand. "Thank you."

"Where to now," Spencer asked as they mounted their horses.

"Hell if I know." Wentworth was beyond frustrated. How could a young lady disappear without a trace? Easy. Servants vanished all the time, and no one ever cared what befell them. Well, this time someone cared and he cared very much.

They were just about to leave when Wentworth heard the servants' door open again and a young girl, around ten or eleven, stepped outside looking nervous. She didn't say a word, just reached inside her soiled apron pocket, reached up, and placed a folded and worn piece of parchment in his hand.

Once again, Wentworth reached inside his pocket and placed two coins in the girl's hand. "Thank you."

Wentworth scanned the paper and tucked it inside his pocket.

"What does it say?" Spencer queried.

"That she is safe, staying with the local midwife."

"Thank God. Let's go get her."

All it took was one inquiry to the first person they came upon on the road, and they knew where the midwife lived. As they approached the small cottage, Wentworth's eyes were drawn to the young girl hanging wash on a line. She hadn't noticed them so he could watch her openly. Her movements and mannerisms reminded him of Bella. Her hair and features were similar to Amelia's. There was no doubt in Wentworth's mind that the girl had told the truth. They shared the same father.

He cleared his throat. "Excuse me miss. I'm Wentworth. Are you by any chance Penelope Sullivan?

The piece of clothing she held fell silently to the ground, she covered her mouth with one hand, and her heart with the other. Tears pooled in her eyes as she nodded her head in response. Eventually she found her voice.

"Yes, Your Grace. I'm Penelope."

Wentworth dismounted and handed the reins to Spencer, who'd also dismounted. Wentworth bowed. "It is a pleasure to make your acquaintance."

"I never really believed you'd come for me."

"Why?"

"Most aristocrats don't care about by-blows."

"Well, I'm not and never will be like most aristocrats. I'm your brother, and you will come home with me and meet your family. They are anxious to make your acquaintance."

"I'm trained as a scullery maid, so I can earn my keep."

"Nonsense. No sister of mine will work. You will be Lady Penelope Seabrook, and I dare any member of the *ton* to question your origins."

That very afternoon Thomas procured a coach and driver, and they headed down the road towards home. Two days later they met up with Smythe, and they had an escort to Stony Cross Manor. Ever since finding Penelope, Thomas had been anxious to get home. Since seeing Smythe and hearing about Sebastian's unfortunate incident and injuries, his anxiety increased tremendously. He would not rest easy until he saw his brother and ascertained he was healthy and well with his very own eyes.

AFTER THE MIDDAY meal when most of the Seabrook family rested in their rooms, Teagan and Lachlan strolled through the formal gardens, which she had to admit were exquisite. The roses were lovely and in full bloom, making her stop and smell each and every different plant much to her brother's chagrin.

"Again," he said as she stopped at a rose an incredible shade of reddish orange.

"Aye, again," she said. "We didnae have gardens nearly this beautiful at home."

"We need tae talk about what Ian confided in ye?" Lachlan said with a somber voice and equally somber expression.

Teagan sighed and answered, "Aye. But ah get the feeling ye already ken the truth."

"Aye, ah had my suspicions. When Maw became ill she had me meet a mon and give him a letter. At the time ah thought he looked familiar, but it took me a day to place him. When we were young children he used tae sit atop his horse at the edge of the forest and watch us. Ah believe he is our real Paw."

"Do ye think he still lives?" God, please let him be alive she prayed.

"Ah dinnae ken. Ah want tae believe he does. And when we are safe we will find out. Meanwhile we have enough tae worry ourselves over."

Teagan had to agree with her brother. But as soon as this thing with Ian and the man she knew as her father were over she would seek out the truth of her real father.

"Something else has been bothering me," Lachlan said with a deep sigh. "Ah keep thinking that Ian is the rightful heir now and not me."

"Not true," Teagan said with conviction. "Maw and the duke were married when we were born and his name is on yer birth record. Ah believe, by law that makes ye his heir. Ye need tae make things right when he dies. The crofters have been suffering for years paying ridiculous rents. They need ye. If Ian became the duke, it would only become worse for them."

"Ah keep telling myself that as well, but ah still have doubts."

"Please try not tae. In any case the duke is still living. Ye can worry later."

"Fine." His lips turned up into a crooked grin. "Dinnae look now, but Lord Sebastian is sitting on a bench looking this way. Ah swear the mon cannae keep his eyes off ye. Nor his hands if what ah witnessed in the drawing room last night was any indication."

She gasped and her face warmed.

"Do ah need tae force him tae ask for ye hand because he compromised ye?"

Words escaped her and mortification took over at knowing her brother witnessed the private scene between her and Sebastian. "L...L...Lachlan, isnae what ye think."

"Relax. When ah approached the doors tae the drawing room last night looking for some brandy tae help me sleep, ah heard both yer voices. Ah left without witnessing anything." He tilted his head and turned serious. "Did he compromise ye? Because if he did..."

"Nay. Nothing like that happened. He kissed me. That is all."

"In our society spending time with a gentlemon in private, without a chaperone and being kissed, is cause for a betrothal." Lachlan said with all seriousness.

"Please, dinnae start thinking like an aristocrat just because we are in England. Ah ken we are aristocrats, but we are more informal in Scotland."

"Thank goodness for that. Being formal all the time gets tiring. Ah keep forgetting tae call Sebastian, Lord Sebastian. It doesnae help that his family is lenient in social etiquette. With that said, I'll leave ye to continue yer examination of the roses. Ah feel the need for an afternoon brandy."

Teagan did not know whether to be thankful he deserted her or not.

"Teagan." The sound of Sebastian saying her name had her insides quaking with anticipation.

"Sebastian."

"Please join me."

As she approached the bench, he scooted over, giving her room. Once she sat down and smoothed out her skirts, she clasped her hands together on her lap and pretended interest in them.

"Do you regret last night?"

His query brought her head up and she studied his face. He looked hesitant and uncertain. How could he possibly be uncertain as to her feelings for him? Because in her mind they were plain as day on her face and in her actions.

"Nay. Do ye?"

"God, no," he said with obvious relief and placed his hand on top of hers. "I will never regret holding you in my arms and kissing you and..."

"Dinnae say it," she blurted out. "Please dinnae say the words. 'Tis bad enough 'tis all ah think about."

"Really?" Now there was amusement in his voice.

"Aye," she said in a whisper.

"Will it make you feel any better if I admit to it being all I think about as well?" And he spoke the truth. When he left Teagan in the hall last night, he'd gone back to his bedchamber, lay in bed and relived the entire encounter over and over again. At breakfast he could hardly keep his eyes off her long enough to take substance.

When he heard her voice talking to her brother moments ago, before the two of them came into view, his heart pounded and he became nervous and hot.

No woman had ever made him nervous before. He'd been so comfortable with Marissa, perhaps that was why they didn't end up married. Comfortable was...well, boring.

Teagan was anything but comfortable. That was not to say they weren't comfortable in each other's company. They were. At least he was. Except there was an undercurrent of attraction and sexual need, want and desire. And excitement and always anticipation, wondering what would happen next.

He desired her like no other. It was all he could think about now, and his body responded in kind. Without giving any consideration to them being seen, he caressed her cheek with the back of his hand, leaned down and brushed her pink lips with his. Her gasp and moan made his decision for him. He turned toward her, placed one hand on the back of her neck, the other on the small of her back, and pulled her in to deepen the kiss. The world around them disappeared. The sound of the birds, the bees, and other bugs went silent. All he heard was their breathing, moaning, and hearts pounding so loud he swore he could not only hear his but Teagan's as well. Her kissing had improved in a short time. When he went to pull back, she curled her hands into his waistcoat and pulled him back to her kiss swollen lips.

When his head tingled and the world spun, he pulled back, wrapped one arm around her waist, and tucked her in close beside him. "I'm afraid if we don't stop, I might start removing your clothing and God knows who might be lurking in the gardens."

He laughed when she gasped and her body tensed. "Relax. I was kidding. We would hear footsteps and voices giving us warning. I heard you and Lachlan long before you came into view and I could see you, but you still didn't have a direct sight to me on this bench, which if you didn't notice, is nicely tucked just off the path."

"And why is that, Lord Sebastian?"

"I would presume the creator of this garden had this very thing in mind. It has been here as long as I can remember."

Teagan sighed and rested her head against his shoulder, making him ache to fold her into his arms and kiss her again.

"We have gardens at Murray Castle, my maw and ah used tae tend them with the gardener. She always said taking care of and loving nature's gifts of life, whatever form it came in, would have rewards. We used some of the special plants and herbs tae make medicine and ointments. Ah used one ah made on yer cuts. Yer leg's gash was deep and nasty, exposing yer bone. Ah thought at one point it might be the death of ye."

Kissing the top of her head he said, "Thank you for saving my life."

"My pleasure."

He chuckled. "Not at first."

"Are ye going tae continue tae bring that up? But aye. Not at first. But when ye opened yer one blue eye, full of pain, confusion, and kindness, ah knew ah'd made the right choice in saving ye."

"I admit looking into your green eyes that first moment sent my world spinning."

She laughed and nudged him with her hip. "Of course ye did. Ye had a skull fracture. Ye were bound tae experience vertigo."

"It was more. Way more than vertigo and I think you know it too."

Before she could reply his lips were upon hers, hot and demanding, causing the world to disappear once again as sensations bombarded his mind, body, and heart.

AFTER HER CHANCE encounter with Sebastian in the gardens, Teagan went to her room and rested before afternoon tea was upon her. The sleepless night spent with Sebastian in the drawing room had left her exhausted, and she took to her comfortable bed. Not long after she lay down, a soft knock sounded on the door and Emma's voice sang out, "May I come in?"

Teagan, not wanting to crush her day dress had rested on top of the covers so she slid her legs over the side, walked toward the door, and opened it. "Aye, please."

Emma bustled in the room, her increasing stomach hardly

slowing her down. She made a beeline to a blue velvet chair facing the hearth. Which at the moment had no fire.

"I'm having a difficult time with the Scottish language in my latest novel. I was hoping you could advise me?"

"Novel?" Teagan queried as she sat in the identical chair beside Emma. "Did ye bring it, so ah can take a look?"

"Let me clarify." Emma smiled. "I am the writer of novels. I'm penning my latest, and I introduced a lovely Scottish lass who speaks like you."

"Writing a novel?" Teagan was shocked at this news. How did the duchess accomplish this? Surely the duke wouldn't approve of her writing novels? The Seabrook family surprised her on a daily basis. They were nothing like she imagined British aristocrats to be. "Could ye explain?"

"Oh, "Emma said with a blush. "When I was in finishing school in Boston I began writing gothic novels. My favorite writer is the author of *Pride and Prejudice*. I fancied myself the next her. Anyway, I write under the name Anna Smith. All the proceeds go to this charity Wentworth and I run for the poor women and children in London."

Teagan didn't know what to say. Emma was an amazing woman. Belonging to an equally amazing family. How had she and Lachlan gotten so lucky as to rescue Sebastian, hence bringing them here to these kind and generous people? Sebastian said fate. Was it fate that brought them together?

She spent the next half hour talking and laughing with Emma. Helping her with the language and succeeding in forgetting her own problems, which she needed. It didn't do Teagan any good to constantly be stressed over her and Lachlan's situation. Sometimes it felt good to let her guard down and enjoy being a young lady.

※

AFTER A LATE DINNER THAT EVENING, Teagan went to her brother's chamber. He had not shown for afternoon tea or dinner and she was worried. Once outside his room she knocked and waited for an answer. When none came she said through the door, "Lachlan, are ye in there?"

"Aye. Come in."

Upon entering the room she noted several things. The brother she spent time with earlier in the day was replaced with an exhausted, pale, and unwell one. He sat by the fireplace, which had a roaring blaze, crystal glass in hand.

"Ah missed ye this evening." She approached his side, put her hand to his forehead, closed her eyes, and said a quick prayer. "Ye are burning up. Why didnae ye send word tae me?"

"Tae tired."

Swallowing her panic, she turned on her healing personality. "Come over tae the bed so ah can examine ye."

"Why."

That got her temper up. "Why? Because ye must get better. Ah need ye. Dinnae ye dare let the duke and Ian win. They havenae killed ye yet. Pretending tae be a coachman and driving us in the foul English weather in the pouring rain has ye sick.

"Dinnae blame England and their inclement weather. 'Tis not as though it doesnae rain in Scotland," he said in a very soft voice which only worried her more.

"Please, let me help ye tae bed?"

"Ah can bloody hell get myself in bed without yer help, thank ye verra much." And he did. Even if seeing him struggle with weakness and dizziness had her hovering beside him every step of the way.

Once he had himself settled on the bed, she went to untie the belt on his dressing robe.

He pushed her hands away. "What are ye doing? Ah'm naked beneath the robe."

"Ah want tae assure myself ye were nae hurt during the confrontation with Ian and his mon. Ye have been acting strange ever since we left the cottage."

"Truly, Ah'm fine. Nay cuts, nay broken bones, nay new gunshot wounds, or stab wounds tae fester and kill me. Just a fever and ah'm a little tipsy."

She tried not to laugh, but she couldn't help herself. He was tipsy. She wasn't sure she'd ever witnessed him in his cups. "Ah'm going tae ring for a servant. Ye need broth and ah need a basin with cool water and a cloth." She paused. "And some of the tonic ah make for fever. Ah have a bottle in my room. Ah'll leave tae fetch it as soon as the servant arrives."

Teagan pulled the tassel and waited, non-too patiently for a servant to arrive. When a young maid came she expressed her concerns for her brother's well-being and asked her to fetch the lady of the house. Then thought better of it. The duchess was with babe and needed her rest. Even more important was what if Lachlan had something contagious. "Could ye ask Lord Sebastian tae come here?"

Teagan hurried to her bedchamber and found the only bottle of medicine she'd packed and then went back to her brother and gave him some.

"That stuff is bloody awful."

"Aye, 'tis, but it works."

A short time later the young maid came back with basin, cloth, and water, and Sebastian on her heels.

"How is he?" he said as he joined her at Lachlan's bedside.

"He is..."

"Until ah die, ah think ah can answer for myself. Ah feel like ah was caught in the stirrups and dragged behind my horse over sharp rocks. Every part of my body aches and ah'm in the fires of hell. That is until the chills set in."

"Ah'll ask ye again why ye didnae ye send for me?"

"Because for this verra reason. Ah dinnae need ye fussing over me."

"Hmm, if nae me, then who? Ah dinnae see a lady in ye life?"

"When was there time? Besides, every eligible female in our village wanted tae marry me. Ah couldnae trust any of them nae tae be working with Paw. Ah could see it, poisoned on my verra wedding night. Ah still keep calling him Paw, even though we ken the truth. Hard tae stop after calling him that my entire life."

"Ah ken. Ah keep calling him Paw. And ah'm sorry, Lachlan."

"What do ye have tae be sorry for? Ye went through yer own nightmare taking care of Maw and then dealing with Paw." He cleared his throat. "Ah called him Paw again. Anyway, ah ken ah said ah cannae wait tae go home. Well, the truth of it is, ah never care if ah see our home again. When and if ah inherit the title, ah think ah'll come tae London, marry a gentle Englishwoman and have a brood of offspring."

"I may be able to help you with the ladies," Sebastian interjected. "Or at the very least, my sisters and Emma could introduce you into London Society. But I have to warn you, being an heir to a dukedom, even one in Scotland, will have every young maiden and her mama after you relentlessly."

"So ah have heard," Lachlan said with soft voice.

Teagan dipped a cloth in the cool water and bathed Lachlan's face and chest. "How does that feel?"

"Heavenly," he replied with closed eyes. Just heavenly."

"Rest."

"Ah'm trying tae but ye keep disturbing me."

Moments later his breathing changed, and Teagan sighed with relief knowing he slept. She prayed the only thing he got from the ride in the rain was a fever and not a cold, or worse, a lung ailment.

"Are you worried?" Sebastian came up behind her and wrapped his arms around her waist. He no longer used the splint on his arm, even though he still favored it. It pleased her to no end having him heal so nicely. And having his arms around her seemed natural, like they'd done it a million times before. Leaning back against his strong, hard chest, she closed her eyes and let herself relax, draining some of the painful tension from her body.

"Aye. Ah wish he'd sent for me when the fever first broke out."

"Men can be stubborn."

That brought a smile to her lips. "Ah never noticed."

"Don't lie. I prefer my women honest."

"Have ye had many women?" The thought of him with other women had her chest tightening.

"Honestly—no." He rubbed his cheek against the top of her head. "I never sowed my wild oats. I don't have the reputation of being a rake."

Pivoting around so she rested her cheek against his chest and her arms wrapped around his waist she said, "Ah never thought ye did...but ah thought all young gentlemen of the *ton* spent their free-time at brothels and their clubs drinking and gambling."

"Many do. But you see, up until my brother married Emma, we were in debt and there wasn't money for drinking and gambling. Not that either one of us would have. Not after my father."

"That's right. Ah forgot. Ah'm sorry."

"Don't start saying sorry."

"Perhaps...you could do something tae keep me from talking?"

His chest shook with laughter. "As much as I would very

much like to kiss you all night long, I won't disrespect your brother that way."

"He's sleeping," she teased and pouted. *Pouted, since when do ah pout? Who have ah become since meeting Sebastian? A woman in love is who. And 'tis wonderful and frightening at the same time.*

"Not here in front of your brother, asleep or not."

"Bet ah could change yer mind?"

"You could, but you won't. Except..." their eyes locked, his were dark with desire and her body inflamed the moment he lowered his head and took her mouth in a mind tingling kiss that left her gasping for air when he stepped back and bowed. "I am retiring for the evening. But before I do, do you need anything else? Should I have someone fetch the local doctor?"

"Ohh." It took a moment for her mind to work. Who knew a kiss could befuddle your brain so. "If his fever hasnae broken by morning, perhaps the physician could be sent for. Until then ah will stay by his bedside."

"Lachlan is fortunate to have you as his sister. Goodnight."

"Goodnight."

The room suddenly dropped in temperature and seemed empty without Sebastian in it. She dragged one of the padded chairs from the fireplace area closer to her brother's bed. Using a spare blanket from the foot of his bed, she wrapped herself in it, and tried to get comfortable.

Sleep didn't come. Listening to Lachlan's uneven breathing and occasional moaning had her concerned. To make him more comfortable and her feel useful, she bathed his face and chest with cool water. He stirred and spoke, but his words were jumbled, only making her more worried. *'Tis just a fever, 'tis just a fever* she kept telling herself. Yes, but people died of from fevers. Not Lachlan.

At some point in the dead of night she must have dosed off because when she awoke the sun was poking through the curtains illuminating a line across the floor. Another telltale sign was her body was stiff and sore from sleeping sitting up.

"Lachlan, are ye awake?"

"Aye. And ah feel surprisingly good."

Standing, Teagan stretched her body, then placed her hand on his forehead. "Nothing short of a miracle. Yer fever is completely gone. Do ye still have the aches and pains?"

Lachlan pulled his robe closed with the sash, sat up and swung his legs over the side of the bed. He sat for a moment and then stood, stretching out his muscles. "Nay. Feel good as new. Thankfully, as ah dinnae have time tae wallow in bed sick."

"Hopefully the duke will be back any day. Meanwhile, sometimes a fever comes back, so my advice tae ye is tae take it easy today. If nothing, then tomorrow ye can go back tae normal."

"Normal? Ah havenae been normal or done normal things since this whole ordeal began."

"Well, perhaps ye can go riding or hunting with Northborough, Bridgeton, and Sebastian in the days tae come."

"Perhaps."

Teagan couldn't help herself, she yawned.

"Please go tae yer room and sleep. Ah'm fine and 'tis still early. Nobody but the servants will be up and about for several hours still."

She kissed her brother on his cheek and made her way to her room. Finding her bed, she climbed beneath the covers fully clothed. Too exhausted to undress or ring for Gretchen's assistance.

CHAPTER THIRTEEN

NOT MUCH CHANGED FOR A SENNIGHT. UNTIL ONE afternoon, as the family gathered in the drawing room enjoying tea and biscuits, there was a ruckus at the door. Sebastian, finally walking without aide of his cane hurried as much as he could into the foyer and was pulled into a big hug by Wentworth.

"It is so good to see you," Wentworth said as he looked him over from head to toe. "I see you're mending well."

"Yes, indeed. Thanks to Teagan and Lachlan Murray."

"So Smythe has told me. Spencer and I seriously need to clean up, and Penelope as well. But I think everyone's anxiety will be appeased if we join you for tea."

It was then that Sebastian looked over his brother's shoulder to where Spencer and Penelope stood looking exhausted from their travels.

"Hello." He bowed. "I'm Sebastian, your brother. Welcome to Stony Cross Manor."

Before she could say anything Wentworth took over the introductions. "Penelope this is our brother, Sebastian. Sebastian this is Penelope.

She curtsied. "Nice to meet you, Lord Sebastian."

"No need to call me lord. Sebastian will do."

"Thank you, kindly."

"Mother must be eager to see us. Let us proceed into the drawing room."

Sebastian stood and watched Wentworth introduce Penelope to the family. She seemed shy, but that was to be expected considering the circumstances surrounding her birth. She resembled Amelia in coloring and height. Mother was being gracious, which couldn't be easy. Albeit, he didn't except anything less from her. She didn't blame the girl for the circumstances of her birth.

Wentworth shared some private words with Lachlan, and Wentworth's eyes never left Sebastian's while Lachlan spoke. Sebastian could only imagine what was being said. Several times his brother winced and his lips moved, no doubt cursing.

Coming his way now, Sebastian braced himself for a tongue-lashing, not that he'd done anything wrong. And he was wrong about the tongue-lashing as Wentworth hugged him close again, surprising him.

"Lachlan filled me in. Bloody hell, you're lucky to be alive...twice. Twice you were beaten. When all is taken care of we will find those highwaymen and Lachlan's brother and string them up."

"Easy brother," Sebastian said. Even though deep down inside he too wished they could string them up. "We can find them but let the authorities deal with their punishment. Didn't you learn anything when Emma was kidnapped by her father's barrister? Rotting in Newgate is a fate worse than death. Just ask Bridgeton, since he spent some time there."

"Yes, well," Wentworth stuttered. "I'd rather not remind Bridgeton of his time in Newgate. We have a rather good relationship now."

"Will you send word to the prince on behalf of the Murrays?"

"First thing in the morning. Also, I want everyone ready to travel to London day after tomorrow." Wentworth glanced across the room, looking directly at Teagan. "Lachlan tells me his sister has fallen for you. Please tell me you have feelings for her and are not just toying with her?"

"Christ, get right to the point, why don't you." Toying with Teagan? Yes, but not toying and stalling. Toying because he couldn't help himself. When they arrived in London and Lachlan had his say to the prince, he would approach Lachlan with his intentions. Which were?

"Sebastian, you didn't answer me." His brother's voice broke into to his reverie.

"No. I'm not toying with her. I think she may be the one."

His brother squeezed his shoulder. "I'm glad. She seems like a lovely woman. And from what Lachlan's told me, she'll keep you on your toes. No meek and biddable woman for you. You would get bored. I hear she hunted the highwaymen alongside her brother. I admire a woman not afraid to act."

"She has much to be admired for. Her compassion, healing skills, and sense of humor for starts."

"Since we've been talking she hasn't taken her eyes off you. Don't mess this up."

"I'll try not to." And he would. He couldn't imagine not being with Teagan on a daily basis. His life would have no purpose without her in it.

TEAGAN DIDN'T KNOW what to think about Wentworth. He may share Sebastian's coloring and eyes, but the similarities ended there. The duke appeared most serious, where Sebastian seldom did. She presumed that came with being raised to be a duke. Much like her brother had been by their mother. But not by their father. Why had they never noticed that? And try as she might she could not be angry at her mother for keeping the truth from them. She was only looking out for their future. Because, undoubtedly, she want Lachlan to inherit.

The young lady who entered the room with them, the long-lost sister, resembled Amelia in hair and eye color. How nervous she must be. The gentleman with them must be the one they called Spencer. Bridgeton's cousin as she understood. There was a stark resemblance between the two of them.

All the gentlemen, her brother included, excused themselves, no doubt they were going to meet in the duke's study.

Penelope, looking tired and disheveled left with the dowager. What must the dowager be thinking upon meeting this child her late husband sired with another woman? Once again she was astonished by the Seabrook family's big hearts.

"She is beautiful and terribly shy. The poor thing must feel lost," Emma said as she poured herself more tea. "Much like I did when I first arrived."

"She looks like Amelia," Bella added.

"A much younger me. She can't be more than ten and six."

"We need to start planning her first Season," Amelia said with a smile. "She will cause quite a stir I believe."

"The Seabrook family is familiar with causing scandal," Bella said.

"I didn't mean scandal, I mean shock the members of the *ton* when we introduce another sister," Amelia clarified with a smile. "I will never forgive some of the *beau monde* for snubbing my husband. But witnessing them grovel now that the real murderer of his brother and sister-in-law was found is entertaining. Of course, he could care less what people think about him. But I want Olivia, and..." she blushed and placed her hand on her belly. "Promise me you can keep a secret, I haven't even told William. Tonight I will. But meanwhile, I can hardly wait to share, I'm expecting. Near to two months as best I can calculate."

Cheers erupted around her. "Shh, I don't want the men running down the hall thinking we're being attacked."

Amelia received hugs and kisses from Emma, Bella, and Teagan.

"Once again our children will be close in age," Emma said with a hand on her own burgeoning belly. Perhaps we will both have sons. A spare for me and an heir for Bridgeton. Wait until he and Olivia find out. They will be thrilled."

"Especially William. He is a wonderful stepfather to Olivia, but he is anxious to have a son or daughter of his own," Amelia said then became quiet.

"Are you not feeling well?" Emma asked. Are you experiencing morning sickness?'

"No. I was just remembering everything William and I have been through."

"It does no good to dwell on the past. All that matters is now. You two are happy, healthy, in love, and have Olivia and another on the way," Bella said. "I can't wait until the day comes when I can tell Myles we're having a baby. He still misses both his father and sister since their deaths, and a baby would bring the sparkle back into his life."

"Any chance you could be now?" Amelia asked a she rubbed her stomach. "It would be wonderful if the three of us were expecting together."

"No. I have my courses. But it can't be long if Myles keeps up with his appetite." Bella blushed. "I can't believe I said that, especially in front of Teagan.

"Why," Teagan asked, having found the conversation interesting to say the least.

"Because you are unmarried and don't have intimate knowledge of the marriage bed," explained Bella."

Now it was Teagan's turn to blush as her cheeks heated. "Weel, actually, my maw told me everything. Ah might nae have experienced it firsthand, but ah ken what happens."

"If your mother said it was a chore to submit to a man's attentions, don't believe it," said Emma. "Not that I had a mother to explain such things to me, but I have heard stories others have told me. When you find the right man for you, you will welcome his advances. You won't have to close your eyes and think happy thoughts as you succumb to his inept fumbling's in the bed if you love each other."

"Has Sebastian," Bella asked with a mischief twinkle in her eyes.

"Bella," Amelia admonished. "I can't believe you asked that?"

"Oh come now," Emma chimed in. "We both know Bella sometimes speaks before she thinks."

"Well?" Bella stated again."

To her own shock Teagan found herself admitting to being kissed. "Sebastian and ah have...kissed more than once."

"Our brother is known for being decent, kind, generous, and un-rakish. I think you two will suit very well." Amelia nibbled on a biscuit. "And after all, you did save his life."

"He doesnae owe me anything. He equally saved mine as weel so we are even."

"Don't you want him beholden to you?" asked Bella

"Nay. Ah want his feelings for me tae have nothing tae do with my saving his life. Besides, ah am betrothed tae a beast of a mon back in Scotland by the name of MacPherson."

"You are?" all of the women said at once.

Teagan hated to even think of Scotland and what befell her and Lachlan there. "Well, my paw betrothed me tae a neighbor, but ah would rather die than surrender tae his ministrations. He already tried tae rape me once…"

Gasps echoed around the room. "What happened?" Bella asked.

Three sets of equally shocked and curious eyes landed on her, making her self-conscious and wishing she'd said nothing. "'Twas the night we escaped for our lives. He tried tae rape me, but ah believe, in his mind, that is how he procreates. The poor women he's been with, and the poor wife he will eventually take because it willnae be me."

"Fortunately for us," Amelia began. "Wentworth believes in love and would never have forced us into marrying for less." She paused then continued. "Except for that time he betrothed me to the Duke of Yarmouth. Although I had agreed. Who knew the man was a degenerate. Thankfully William found us in the gardens as he tried to force his attentions on me."

"Some men can be brutal. Thank God not ours," Emma said. "Although when I first met Wentworth I truly didn't like him. I resented him and thought him stuffy and overbearing. Secretly, I couldn't take my young, innocent eyes off him and thought I could make that scowl disappear off his face. Who knew I really could. Of course, Myles traveled with us and we flirted shamelessly. As the ship got closer and closer to England, I thought steam would come out of Thomas's ears. He was so bad tempered he actually growled at us numerous times during the crossing." Emma paused to take a sip of her tea.

"Of course I didn't realize Myles was flirting to get over Sophia LeFluer from New Orleans, who he believed he'd fallen in love with and dueled with her affianced...I'm sorry Bella. I should not have said that."

Teagan's head spun with all these revelations. "Ah dinnae understand."

Bella shrugged her shoulders. "When my brother traveled to America to get Emma, Myles accompanied him. They spent the year getting Emma's father's affairs in order. Well, my brother did. Myles traveled the country. He met a French woman on a paddleboat on the Mississippi River and became enamored with her. He dueled her intended and unbeknownst to him the man died shortly after from infection. She traveled two years later to enact her revenge on Myles. Sophia married Myles's cousin, Gerard, and they schemed to kill him so Gerard could inherit as he was next in line. One night they tried to poison me, for fear I carried the heir." Bella's eyes watered. "They killed Myles's sister, Catherine, by mistake."

"Oh my God. How tragic." Teagan gasped. So she wasn't the only family with scheming relatives who had no morals.

"It was. Then they poisoned Myles but miscalculated the dose and he, thank God, survived. Sophia died from rat poison as well, thanks to Gerard, who is rotting in Newgate."

"And ah thought my family has been through quite a bit," Teagan said.

"You have," Bella said, with Amelia and Emma agreeing. "But look at us now? We have persevered, married the men of our dreams and heart. You will too."

Teagan wasn't convinced just yet that her dreams would come true. And what were her dreams? Did she love Sebastian and hope for her very own happy-ever-after as her new found friends had? Her heart did a little leap inside her chest.

Perhaps when things got settled with her family. Thinking about Lachlan pained her so. He should be living a carefree, bachelor life. Instead he was running for his life. Father should have sent him to court, he should have had a London Season, danced at balls and soirees, and attended Almack's. Instead he was forced to remain in Scotland at their father's beck and call. Not their real father. She had to keep remembering that.

Perhaps he could attend next Season and find his future duchess. Mayhap she could have a Season as well, even though she already found the man she wanted to wed. She had always secretly dreamed of having one. But she had been busy taking care of the infirm and then her mother. But now that she met Emma, Bella, and Amelia, a Season might be fun. Besides, dancing a waltz with Sebastian would be heaven.

TWO DAY HENCE, she traveled in a carriage with Lachlan, Wentworth, and Emma. As they approached London, Teagan did not know where to look first. She craned her neck and looked out the window at all the hustle and bustle happening around them.

"Ah havenae seen so many people or carriages. What part of London are we in?"

"Mayfair," Wentworth answered. Our home is just up the street a ways."

Home was a strange word for the enormous red brick manor they pulled up to with wrought iron fencing, lush green lawns, and numerous gardens. Lachlan helped her down from the carriage and up the stairs into a large foyer where a row of servants greeted them.

Next thing she knew, she was being led up the grand staircase by her newly appointed lady's maid, down a hall and then another and led into the most beautiful room she'd ever seen. Murray Castle had its charm, but in a rustic country way. Her room at Stony Cross Manor was beautiful. This room was even more so, done up in subtle shades of blue, yellow, and cream. A fire blazed in the hearth, and she longed to relax on the chaise with a good book.

The four poster bed was covered in a blue and cream paisley damask coverlet which looked inviting to her travel weary body.

"Would you care to change before going down for tea, milady? Your trunk arrived this morning, and I took the liberty of unpacking the contents."

Not her trunk. Not her clothing. Everything belonging to her could be found back at Murray Castle. A case of melancholy had her heading to the chaise and sitting down on it before her legs gave way. Tears clogged her throat. She missed her mother. She'd never really had a proper time to mourn her loss and something about this room and the Seabrook family had her aching for her mother. None of this would be happening if she still lived. Tears sprinkled down her cheeks, and she hugged herself as a chill settled deep insides her bones even with the roaring blaze in the hearth.

"Would you like some privacy, milady? I can return shortly."

"Aye, please."

When the door clicked closed, Teagan curled up on the chaise and let herself cry, really cry for the first time since her mother passed and she and Lachlan had run for their lives. Deep painful sobs rose up from the depth of her soul, shaking her body uncontrollably.

Eventually her sobs turned to silent tears, and she closed her eyes and succumbed to the exhaustion that had plagued her since Scotland.

"Teagan, my dear daughter, sit with me a spell."

Teagan had just finished breakfast and went to check on her mother to see if she felt any better. With one glance at her pale, drawn face and blue tinged lips, Teagan had her answer. She swallowed the lump in her throat and pasted on a smile. It wouldn't do to have her mother see how concerned she was for her health. Terrified was more like it because her mother looked on death's door.

She rested her hip on her mother's bed and took her chilled hands in hers, hoping to share some of her warmth with her. "How are ye feeling today?"

"Ah fear the end is near and ah must tell ye something." Her mother inhaled, then spoke so softly Teagan found herself leaning close in order to hear.

"Ye and Lachlan will be in danger when ah'm gone."

This shocked her. In danger? "Maw, why?"

"Yer paw will marry ye tae that brute of a mon MacPherson once ah'm dead. Ye must leave here the moment ah take my final breath. Also, Lachlan's life is in danger. Yer paw will have him killed so Ian can inherit. Yer real paw...never mind. Promise me when ah die ye will nae stay for my burial. Ye and Lachlan will run tae my father and brothers. They will protect ye.

"Maw. Ye are talking nonsense."

Her mother's fingers gripped hers with surprising strength. "Ah am speaking the truth. Pack now and be ready tae leave. Talk tae yer brother. Ye must both be ready as my time approaches."

Teagan didn't have a chance to speak to Lachlan because minutes later their mother took her last breath and went into God's hands.

"Maw," Teagan cried out and sat up, shaking from her dream. She lay back down, and when her breathing slowed and turned normal, she strolled across the room and pulled the bell pull.

Moments later her maid came in the room. "Milady."

"Please, would ye help me dress? Ah fear ah'm late for tea."

Twenty minutes later with Prissy's help, she found her way to the downstairs drawing room where tea was still being served. She only hoped she didn't scare away anyone with her swollen, red rimmed eyes.

The gentlemen, per usual, stood across the room in a circle having a serious discussion. Emma, Amelia, and the dowager sat on the settee while Bella sat on a burgundy velvet chair facing them. Teagan sank her weary body in the matching chair beside it. Poor Penelope was not there. No doubt she was in her room mourning her mother as Teagan had been.

"May I pour you tea?" Bella offered.

"Aye, please."

Bella fixed it with two sugars and extra cream, just the way she preferred it. She also put two frosted teacakes on a plate.

"Thank ye."

"You look tired, my dear." The dowager observed over her china teacup. Perhaps you should rest before the evening meal. Or better, take a tray in your room. You've been through a terrible ordeal. Things will improve for you and Lachlan now that Wentworth is back and we have arrived in London."

"Ah'll admit ah'm a little tired, although ah did just dose off for a spell. It isnae physical exhaustion, but mind and spirit."

"Yes, well, as I've said, you've been through a terrible ordeal," the dowager added.

"Thank ye for yer hospitality, Yer Grace."

"I think I speak for everyone, including Wentworth, when I say you are most welcome to stay as long as you need a home. Lachlan as well. Although I imagine he is chomping at the bit to seek vengeance and fight for his birthright."

And there lay the problem. Teagan was petrified he would go and fight for what was his and end up dead. Oh, dear, she would not cry again. What a watering pot she'd turned into lately. It was time for the stubborn, determined, and independent woman she'd always been to come back to her. She pushed her shoulders back. If she appeared to have backbone, perhaps she would.

"That does worry me. Lachlan can be a bit bullheaded at times. Act before he thinks things through clearly."

Bella reached over and squeezed her hand. "Our men will not let him go off half-cocked searching for a fight."

"Bella, such language," her mother admonished.

"I'm sorry. Forgive me. But all of you get my point. Lachlan is much like Wentworth in that regard."

"Yes, indeed, he is," Emma chimed in. "But do not fret Teagan. He is not alone in his fight. Wentworth has already sent word to the prince. I expect we will receive a message from him post-haste."

"It will be a relief tae have his assistance."

"Priney, for all his faults, is a good man. He and my son have had their differences over the years, but they have remained close."

"Differences?" Teagan couldn't resist asking. Everything she'd learned about the Seabrook's so far was more than interesting.

"There was that one time he wanted Wentworth to marry the daughter of a Scottish Earl to improve relations with Scotland. He married our dear Emma instead. Priney refused to attend the nuptials. But all was forgiven when next they were in each other's company," the dowager said.

"It took courage tae go against the prince's wishes," Teagan remarked, wondering who this daughter of a Scottish Earl was.

"Wentworth's quite arrogant at times, and he would never have married to appease the prince even if he hadn't fallen in love with our Emma," the dowager said with a smile to her daughter-in-law.

"Thank you," Emma replied with a blush.

"More tea?" Bella said to Teagan after noticing her cup was empty.

Funny, she hardly remembered drinking it. "Aye, please." She glanced over her shoulder, wondering what the men were discussing in soft voices.

CHAPTER FOURTEEN

WHEN DOES SMYTHE LEAVE FOR SCOTLAND?" SEBASTIAN asked as he noticed Teagan looking their way.

"Aye, when?" Lachlan asked as well.

"On the morrow. He is not to approach your father or Ian. Only to investigate. Also, he is sending men to Dunbar Castle in hopes the laird has word about your relatives since they are distant cousins of his and reside on land near his on the Lothian Coast. We need all the information we can get before we ask the prince to send his soldiers." He paused. "Priney is extremely busy and cannot meet with you and Teagan in person, but I assure you he is abreast of the situation and he advised all of us to wait until Smythe reports in. I'm hoping we can settle it without the help of soldiers."

"There is one more matter ah would like tae have Smythe address," Lachlan said.

"I'm listening." Wentworth stopped and took a sip of tea. "Blasted, this stuff is cold already. Myles, will you be kind enough to get us some brandy."

"Our paw isnae really our paw. Ah would like tae ken who is? He is English."

"Done. I'll send a message. Meanwhile Myles has agreed to host a gathering in your and Teagan's honor. The official Season may be over, but there are plenty members of the *ton* left in London, and they are probably most bored and will welcome a ball."

"That isnae necessary," Lachlan said.

Myles approached, juggling glasses of brandy. Sebastian plucked one of the glasses out of his hand and took a large sip, enjoying the blissful burn. His ears were still ringing from Lachlan's words about their father.

"I think it a splendid idea. Waiting for news from Smythe will go by much faster with things to do," Myles chimed in."

"That's why I asked Myles and Bella to host the ball. Of course," Wentworth said as he took a generous sip of his drink. "Myles's sisters were just as happy to have something to occupy their time while they anxiously await word from Marissa."

"Speaking of Marissa," Sebastian said with a frown. "No word yet?"

Myles swore as he downed his drink in one gulp. "Bloody hell. Not a word. Does she not know we are worried and most anxious to welcome her husband into the family? We don't care if she ran off to Gretna Green, we just want her safe and happy. And if her captain makes her happy, then we're happy too."

"Perhaps she will be home in time for the ball, and it can be given in their honor instead of mine and Teagan's," Lachlan said over his glass. "Ah think ah speak for Teagan as weel when ah say we prefer nae tae be made a fuss over."

Myles slapped him on the back. "Too bad. This is London, and we love a good excuse to get drunk, dance, and behave badly."

"Seriously?"

"Some of it." Myles shrugged his shoulders.

Out of the corner of his eye, Sebastian saw Teagan excuse herself and quietly leave the drawing room. He could hardly take his eyes off her swaying hips.

Wentworth cleared his throat and tilted his head in the direction of the door.

Really? He wanted him to follow her. Well, hell, who was he to ignore his brother.

After excusing himself, he made his way out into the foyer and caught a glimpse of Teagan's light blue skirts at the top of the staircase.

Taking two stairs at a time, he caught up with her in the hallway outside her bedchamber door.

"Teagan," he gasped as he reached her. "Are you ill?"

"Nay. Ah just...ah dinnae ken what ah am. Please excuse me Sebastian."

Before she could shut the door he pushed his way inside, closed the door behind him, and watched as she strolled over to the fireplace, hug herself and rub her upper hands as if she were chilled.

He sighed deeply as he moved behind her and wrapped his arms around her waist, pulling her close to his body. At first she tensed, then she relaxed back against him and he breathed a sigh of relief.

"Tell me what's wrong."

"Nothing's wrong. Ah just feel lost. Ah was doing fine until we arrived here today. And then suddenly Ah felt out of control of my emotions."

He caressed the top of her head with his cheek. "When Wentworth and I had our fight over Emma and I left for America, my emotions were not easy to control. For a year I thought someone else possessed my body. I'm not saying I didn't enjoy my time away, or that I wasn't responsible for my actions, it's just it seemed like I was looking down at myself.

And then Amelia showed up broken hearted and expecting... Perhaps I shouldn't have said that."

"Forgive me, but ah dinnae understand."

"Olivia's real father, Captain Rycroft, Amelia's betrothed died weeks before their wedding in a hunting accident. Leaving her pregnant and frightened and on the verge of ruin."

"Thank goodness she found such a good man in her earl. He truly loves her."

This time he didn't run his cheek along the top of her head, instead he inhaled deeply of her rose scented hair. What he wouldn't give to pluck each and every pin from her glorious hair and slide his fingers through her long red tresses, which would no doubt, cascade down to her narrow waist. Then, of course, he'd work on the little pearl buttons and divest her of her clothing.

"Sebastian?"

"Apologies," he murmured into her hair when he realized he'd flexed his hips, pushing his erection into her backside and she obviously felt it. How could she not as it was full to near bursting from his breeches.

"No need."

Was she giggling? Her body was shaking ever so slightly. Or perhaps crying. His muscles tensed as he turned her around, and instantly he relaxed when he observed her silently laughing.

"What, pray tell, is so humorous?"

"Nothing. I've just never had a mon's swizzle stick, for a better word, pressed and seeking against my...behind."

Sebastian smiled down at her and wondered how she felt now that it was shoved up against her stomach...hard and seeking. He didn't dwell on it. He lowered his head and took her soft, full lips in a sensual kiss that soon turned desperate and all consuming. His blood boiled and he had to touch her.

While continuing to plunder her mouth, he rejoiced in the little breathy noises she made and the feel of her hands clutching the front of his waistcoat. He proceeded to unbutton the top several buttons on her dress so he could tug it down, exposing her breasts to his touch. Unfortunately her hands were in the way and needed to be moved. He gently pried her fingers from his coat, wrapped them around his waist, and tugged the front of her gown down, taking her chemise with it.

Finally her breasts fell full and heavy into his hands and he groaned into her mouth. Then he dropped his head and took one of her nipples into his mouth.

"Sebastian."

"Mmm, you taste delicious."

"We shouldnae."

He paused and waited, praying she wouldn't halt him.

"Dinnae stop."

He chuckled against her creamy smooth skin and bit down lightly on her nipple and she gasped.

"Sebastian."

Sebastian good? Or Sebastian bad?

The way she clutched his head to her breast, he'd take that as good. He moved his attentions to her twin then slowly dropped to his knees and kissed his way down her body, moving aside clothing that got in his way, exposing her lovely skin.

One arm caressed its way up her calf, then thigh seeking the slit between her pantaloons and the core of her womanhood.

Teagan's moans encouraged him to continue on his quest. He'd touched her there before, but this time he planned on tasting her as well. But first...he scooped her up into his arms and carried her to the bed, depositing her gently on the fluffy coverlet all the while never taking his eyes off hers. If he saw any hesitancy in her eyes, he'd stop and leave the room posthaste.

When all he saw was lust in her glassy green eyes, his heart accelerated and his hands suddenly shook from the magnitude of her trust in him.

"Teagan," he murmured as he raised her skirts and slowly lowered her pantaloons. "I want to taste you, will you let me?"

"Taste?" she asked with a breathy voice that had his lust spiking even more.

"Do you trust me?"

"Aye."

"Then I promise you will enjoy my tasting of you. But I vow to you here and now, I will not take your innocence." Not today anyway. He had to be one hundred percent convinced of a future with her before he would risk a child on her. He knew he wanted her as his wife, but there was a small problem back in Scotland that needed to be solved first. The problem of a betrothed Scot.

Looking at her now with her skirts bunched around her waist, her lovely breasts bare, nipples pink and puckered had his hands trembling. What had he ever done to deserve Teagan looking at him with desire and trust in her eyes? Please God, let him be worthy.

His quivering hands moved up her bare thighs, parting her legs, revealing moist curly hair. He brushed his fingers across her womanhood, causing a soft moan from Teagan to reach his ears. He lowered his head and tasted her. A groan escaped him at her exquisite flavor. Using his tongue, his teeth and mouth he had Teagan undulating into his mouth. Her hips rose off the bed urging him to continue.

"Sebastian...ah...dinnae think ah can..."

"Relax and enjoy. Listen to your body and let nature work its wonder."

She did because when he slipped one finger inside her, her

inside muscles clenched and pulsed around his finger. He kept it inside her but rose up and kissed the screams from escaping her mouth.

Moments later, he pulled her pantaloons up, pushed her skirts down and righted her bodice, then pulled her into his arms and held her close to his heart.

"Why don't you rest? I'll leave soon."

"Sebastian, what we did. Do ye think badly of me?"

Her words and the way she expressed them eviscerated his heart.

"My dear, Teagan." He kissed the top of her head. "I could never think badly of you. Besides, do you honestly believe I would compromise you in my family's home if I didn't love you?"

TEAGAN COULD HARDLY BREATHE. Sebastian loved her? He loved her. When he walked into her room behind her and shut the door she didn't know what to expect. She knew he cared for her and had taken liberties before. But in her bedchamber?

Did she stop him from making advances? No. Because she loved him. In many ways he reminded her of Lachlan. Honest, loyal, and kind to a fault. He'd shared confidences with her and she him. Secrets that only seemed natural to share.

Being with him made her insides hum and throb. In an, *ah am alive* kind of way. Not in her wildest dreams did she think, when they escaped their father's clutches, she would ever find happiness. Never mind love. And now she found herself curled up within the strong arms of the man who loved her and her him. And what they shared only moments ago would not make her ashamed. Not with the man she loved.

Her hand rested on his heart, which beat a tad faster than normal. "I love you."

His chest rose and fell, which she presumed was relief on his part. She leaned up and kissed his mouth. "Ah'm going tae rest now if 'tis fine with ye."

His arms tightened around her. "Sleep. I've got you. No one will ever hurt you again. Not with me and my family to keep you safe."

Feeling the rise and fall of Sebastian's chest and hearing the steady beat of his heart lulled her to sleep.

In her dreams her mother still lived and was healthy. She and Lachlan were about nine and running around the lush lawn chasing butterflies. Laughter and happiness surrounded them, but she knew it was rare to experience such happiness. Father was mean. Even to Mother, which to Teagan's young mind, was hard to understand. Mother was beautiful and kind, how could Father be unkind to her? Even hateful at times. And why did he seem to love Ian but was short of temper around her and Lachlan?

Today their father took Ian on a hunt, which displeased Mother. A hunt was no place for a boy of eight.

Teagan was silently glad Ian was with Father. Her younger brother was pushy and mean. He hurt the stray kittens that lived in the stables. Enjoyed catching toads and pulling off their legs.

Today she and Lachlan could catch butterflies without risking Ian tearing off their wings and killing them. Find toads and grasshoppers without risking their lives.

"Maw, Teagan look what ah found." Lachlan scooped up a large toad into his hands and ran over to show them.

"Be gentle, my boy. 'Tis one of God's creatures and should be treated kindly."

"Ah wouldnae hurt him like Ian does."

"We will nae spoil our day thinking about yer brother.

Today is our day," Mother said as she ruffled Lachlan's unruly hair. Then she gasped and looked almost frightened.

Teagan followed her mother's eyes and found a man close by on horseback watching them. He tipped his hat, smiled, but didn't come any closer. Yet even from this distance Teagan could see the man appeared sad. His smile didn't reach his eyes.

"Maw, who is that?" Teagan placed her hand into her mothers who suddenly looked sad as well.

"A gentlemon ah knew a longtime ago."

"Why are ye crying?"

Her mother wiped her tears away. "Because ah miss him. We were once good friends. His wife passed many years ago and ah think he is lonely."

"Perhaps he could take tea with us?"

"Nay. That would nae be proper with yer paw gone."

When Teagan looked again, the man had vanished as if he was never there at all, and she wondered why he didn't speak to them.

One night she heard loud voices coming from her mother's chambers. Father was shouting about seeing him. And if he ever saw him on his property again, he would shoot him dead. Teagan didn't have to wonder who he was. It was the man who watched them from afar. Sometimes she dreamed that he loved their mother and would take them all away from here, from Father.

Their voices escalated. Mother screamed if he killed him, she would take Ian and he'd never see his son again. Hearing her mother's words made Teagan afraid. If Mother left with Ian, would she leave her and Lachlan behind?

Over the next several months Teagan saw the man on the edge of the forest watching. One day she approached the stranger and told him what her father had said.

The man looked unhappy but proud sitting on top of his large mount. "Your paw will never kill me, young Teagan."

"Why do ye watch us?"

"Because I need to know you, Lachlan, and your mother are safe."

"Why wouldnae we be?" Even as she asked the question, she knew with Paw's temper they were not safe. Not if the way he backhanded Lachlan two days ago and gave him a split lip was any indication.

"I knew your father many, many years ago."

"He is mean."

The stranger's lips set in a grim line. "Yes, he is. If something ever happens to your mother, you and Lachlan must flee Murray Castle immediately. Travel to your grandfather and uncles. They will welcome you and keep you safe."

"Can we nae come tae ye?"

"Sweet child. I wish that more than anything else in the world. But things being as they are, it will never happen. Be happy and safe my dear child. Know you are loved."

"Wait!" Teagan sat up, startled from her dream. How could she have forgotten about the mysterious stranger? Perhaps Lachlan telling her about him had her remembering. It all made sense to her now. She now believed the stranger to be her and Lachlan's father. So where was he, and why didn't he come for them when Mother died?

"Teagan, you were dreaming. Crying out in your sleep," Sebastian said with concern.

She rested back down and sighed. She told Sebastian about her dream. Only it really wasn't a dream, she was reliving times from her childhood.

"Do you believe he is your real father?"

"Aye. Only ah dinnae ken his name or where he's from. Ah only know he is English. Ah never put that together until now. A titled gentlemon ah believe. Do ye think ah will ever learn the truth about him?"

"Perhaps one day you will."

After Sebastian left her room, she summoned her maid to help her dress for the evening meal. On her way, she stopped by her brother's room and quietly knocked on the door and waited.

"Come in."

Teagan entered her brother's bedchamber just as she heard the supper bell and found him struggling to tie his neck cloth. "Here, let me." She shooed his hands aside and concentrated on tying a simple knot. One her mother taught her in case her future husband's valet was ever indisposed and he needed her assistance. To Teagan's way of thinking, teach the men to tie their own cravat and then they wouldn't need help.

"Dinnae Maw ever teach ye tae tie one of these? She taught me."

Lachlan laughed. "She tried, but ah'm all thumbs."

"There." She stepped back and observed her twin. He stood quite a bit taller than she, he was lean and handsome, but they shared the same color hair and eyes. There was an innate gentleness about her brother. Yet she knew he could be fierce when need be. He'd proved it the night they ran for their lives.

"Ah had a dream about the mon who used tae watch us from afar."

Lachlan turned serious. "Ah neglected tae tell ye about the day ah handed him Maw's note when she'd taken ill. Tae be honest, ah wasnae hospitable tae him. By then ah'd figured out he was our paw and ah was angry at him."

"Ye thought he was our paw then and never said anything tae me?"

"Aye. Sorry. He dinnae confirm or deny it when ah asked.

But ah could see it in his eyes. What ah still dinnae understand is why Maw dinnae just marry him?"

"He was married," Teagan said. "Ah remember Maw telling us, the first time we saw him, when we were around nine that his wife had recently passed."

"Poor Maw, tae have fallen in love with a married mon. No wonder she married Paw. She was ruined. But couldnae Grandpaw have picked someone nicer?" Lachlan said.

"Ah believe Paw played everyone for a fool. He wanted Maw's money. He'd do anything for it and he did. And Ah'm quite sure Grandpaw was pleased to have Maw marry a duke."

"No wonder he hates us and wants Ian tae inherit."

"We need tae find him? Ah want tae ken who he is." Not for the first time did she think about finding their real father and learning the truth of the past.

"First, let's deal with Paw...the duke, and Ian, then find him."

"Lachlan." She had the overwhelming need to hug him close to her heart. "Please dinnae let anything happen tae ye. Ye'r all the family ah have left."

He wrapped his arms around her. "Same here."

"There's something else ah want tae tell ye."

"Aye."

"Ah'm in love with Sebastian."

"Ah ken."

She pulled back and looked at his smiling face. "How?"

"One look at ye when he is in the room and anyone would be blind nae tae see the love shining from yer eyes."

"Oh, God, really?" Now she was mortified. Was she that obvious with her emotions?

"Dinnae fret. He looks at ye the same."

"He does?" She could not help the smile that graced her lips.

"Aye, sister, he does. He is a good mon and will make ye happy and a good husband."

"He will...that is if he asks," she said with a sudden hope."

"He will. Trust me on this."

"We are getting ahead of ourselves. He hasnae asked me tae marry him. Besides, ah couldnae possibly marry anyone until things are settled with ye. Ah need tae ken ye are safe and happy. We need tae find ye a wife."

His chest shaking with laughter had her frowning at him.

"Is the thought of ye married funny?" Teagan asked as laughter tried to overtake her frown.

"Nay. Ah just dinnae see it happening anytime soon. Besides, ah must meet a young lady first, and our life hasnae exactly been conducive tae courting ladies."

"Perhaps now that we are in London, ye might find that special young lady who steals yer heart."

"Perhaps, but ah'm nae holding my breath. Ah'll die if ah do. We must go before we are late for dinner."

CHAPTER FIFTEEN

THE SOIRÉE HELD AT THE NORTHBOROUGH ESTATE WAS Teagan's first experience with London Society. It may be considered the Little Season, but one would never know by the amount of guests attending. She barely managed to breathe with her heart pounding so heavily, crushing her lungs. She ascended the stairs and stood waiting in the receiving line to pay her respects to her hosts, Myles and Bella. As she waited, she noticed quite a few people looking her way. Perhaps they were looking at Sebastian since he escorted her. She smiled and bowed graciously to Myles and Bella and then Sebastian guided her into the magnificent gold ballroom. The flickering lights from the chandeliers cast shadows, making the large room appear cozy.

"Would you care for some refreshments before the orchestra begins playing?" Sebastian said with a grin. "By the many glances you are receiving, I believe you will be hard pressed to find freedom between the sets. Which brings to mind, please pencil me in for the first waltz, so I don't become jealous."

"Done." She smiled, hoping she could contain her nervous

excitement for the entire night. When she'd turned seventeen, her mother had begged her father to let her have a Season. Mother had wanted to bring both her and Lachlan to London so they could mingle with people of their own class. Father refused. He said he'd never set foot on London soil and if it was good enough for him, it was good enough for his children.

Teagan had been devastated because she knew it meant she would marry some backwoods country gentleman. Or in reality, a Scottish Laird.

"Ah dinnae feel like my usual self tonight," she admitted.

"Why? You look stunning and those gentlemen over in that corner keep looking over this way. If it keeps up, I'll have to defend your honor."

She stifled a laugh with her hand. "Ah doubt it. But truly, please dinnae leave my side." She turned her head this way and that. "Ah havenae seen my brother since we arrived. Do ye see him?"

"Over there." Sebastian pointed. "Talking to Lord Bradbury."

"Perhaps we could join him."

Lord Bradbury's eyes followed her movements as she crossed the ballroom, making her nerves tingle and a face from her past flash before her eyes. The face of the mysterious stranger from the woods. The love of her mother's life. How did he come to be here tonight of all nights? Yesterday she said she wanted to find him, but now that he was here, she was nervous and hesitant.

"Teagan," Lachlan said looking far too serious. "May ah present Lord Bradbury? Lord Bradbury, this is my sister, Lady Teagan.

Bradbury took her hand and bowed deeply. "It is an honor to finally be formally introduced."

She curtsied. "The honor is all mine. Ah now have a name tae go with yer face."

Lachlan looked from her to Bradbury and back to her, then addressed Sebastian. "Do ye think Myles would mind if we commandeered a room for privacy. There is something Lord Bradbury would like tae discuss with Teagan and myself."

"Not at all. I know the estate well. I'll see you to one of the small parlors on this level."

Once inside a lovely cream and gold room, Sebastian lit several oil lamps. Stirred the embers in the fireplace, causing a nice large flame to ignite, then left closing the doors quietly behind him.

"Thank you for agreeing to speak with me," Lord Bradbury said. "Please sit, this may take some time."

Teagan sat on a gold brocade settee while Lachlan and Bradbury took chairs facing her. She had the feeling this conversation would change her life forever. For the better she hoped with all her heart.

"First I must apologize for meeting you under these circumstances. I had planned on calling upon Wentworth Manor on the morrow. But when I knew you both would be attending this evening, I could not wait. Yet I still find myself at a loss."

"For whatever reason, my lord?" Teagan asked although she knew.

"Please keep an open mind with what I have to tell you both. I'm not asking for forgiveness, just understanding that what happened long ago was unavoidable and broke both your mother's heart and mine."

Was Teagan finally ready to hear the facts pertaining to her mother and Lord Bradbury's past? The honest answer could only be yes. She was beyond ready to learn the truth to all their pasts.

"When your mother and I met many years ago, we fell in love. I had no business falling in love with her as I was affianced to another."

"Please, get tae the point," Lachlan said quite angrily.

"To my understanding, you never knew the man who raised you was anything but your real father until recently, according to Wentworth. What I want you both to know is I'm your real father."

"Oh," was all Teagan could say to hearing the words spoken out loud. She leaned back against the settee and studied the man who just admitted to being her father.

There were similarities to Lachlan and Bradbury. Their height and eyes mostly.

"Please let me start from the beginning. I became Viscount Bradbury when I was twenty. The very year I met your mother. Unfortunately, because of bad investments my father made, my family was broke. The only way I could support my mother and three younger sisters was to marry for money." He paused and exhaled.

"As much as it devastated both of us, your mother understood. She was an heiress herself, but we never discussed me breaking my betrothal. It wasn't until after my marriage that your mother realized she was with child. By then it was too late."

Teagan sought out her brother and they exchanged wide-eyed looks.

"Why did ye watch from the edge of the forest when we were young?" Teagan asked, although she knew the answer.

"I tried to stay away, but you see, my wife died in childbirth as did my son. I wanted so desperately to acknowledge you both as mine, but I knew your father would kill you three before letting you go."

"He would have," Lachlan said with a frown.

"When your mother took ill, and you gave me the letter,

Lachlan, I was devastated. When no word came for several months I traveled to Murray Castle and had words with your father. He threw me out. Said I would never see either of you again and that your mother had passed that very morning.

I left, not knowing what else to do. I went back to London brokenhearted. I hired an investigator who later informed me you were both guests of the Duke of Wentworth. Which to my utter delight, gave me hope to call upon you there. I wanted to explain how very sorry I was for what I'd done and for the loss of your mother."

Ever since Teagan had found out the truth about her parentage, she'd wondered what her real father was like. She rather envisioned him as a modern day prince. Although not a prince, per say, Bradbury was handsome enough to be one. He seemed kind and gentle of heart, and she could understand why her mother fell in love with him.

"Paw tried tae kill Lachlan, and he gave me tae a barbarian by the name of MacPherson tae marry."

"I am sorry. I should have been a better man where your mother was concerned."

"Did ye love her?" Teagan held her breath as she waited for his answer, praying he said yes.

He didn't hesitate. "Yes, very much. The love your mother and I shared is not a love that would ever die. I will love her until I join her."

Lachlan jumped up and began pacing. "Why are ye confessing all now? Tae ease yer conscience?"

Teagan didn't blame her brother for his anger. Deep down she was angry as well. Angry at circumstances that kept two people who loved each other from being together and happy. Angry that her mother was dead. Angry that Bradbury had not been the father who raised her.

"No. I'm telling you because it's time you knew the truth."

"The truth?" Lachlan yelled as he stood looking down at

Bradbury. "Ye left my mother tae marry a monster who hated us. Made our lives miserable for what? Money?"

"Lachlan," Teagan warned. "Calm down, please."

He spun her way. "Calm down? Calm down? He has no idea what our life was like or Maw's."

"I bed to differ," Bradbury interjected. "Your mother and I corresponded regularly."

Lachlan spun his way. "And that is supposed tae make me feel better?"

"No. I deserve your anger and more. All I'm asking is a chance to make it up to you both. To keep you safe."

A gentle knock on the door had Lachlan calling out, "Come in."

"Excuse me," Bella said as she stepped inside the room dressed splendidly in deep blue silk. "Sebastian asked me to check on you. Is everything fine?"

"Lady Northborough." Bradbury stood and bowed. "A pleasure to see you again. I believe the three of us are done with our conversation for the time being. If you wouldn't mind paying my respects to Northborough, I will take my leave."

"Lady Teagan, Lord Lachlan." Bradbury bowed. "Until we speak again."

"What was that about?" Bella asked, looking shocked at Bradbury's abrupt departure.

"Nothing," Lachlan said as he too quit the room.

"Well," Bella said. "Shall we rejoin the others?"

"Oh, Bella," Teagan said as tears pooled in her eyes. "Ah'm afraid ah cannae possibly make pleasant conversation and pretend everything is fine even if 'tis my first ball. Ah think ah would like tae go home."

❄

As the carriage took Teagan, Lachlan, and Sebastian back to Wentworth Manor, Sebastian wondered not for the first time what had transpired between Bradbury, Teagan, and Lachlan. Teagan had wanted him to stay at the ball and dance, but he couldn't when he knew she was hurting.

Perhaps when they arrived home, one of them would confide in him. For all that he didn't really know Bradbury, he'd never heard anything remotely scandalous about him. After the death of his wife many years ago, he became something of a recluse. Albeit a recluse in London. Occasionally, he would attend a social function and then disappear for another year before he would surface again.

People attributed it to his heartbreak from his wife and infant son's deaths. Perhaps that wasn't it at all. Sebastian was determined to find out the connection between Bradbury and his carriage companions. Could he be their real father?

The silence didn't end as they entered Wentworth Manor and handed over their greatcoats, hats, and pelisse to the doorman.

"Can I have a private word with you Lachlan?" Sebastian asked.

"Nae tonight. Perhaps tomorrow," Lachlan answered as he climbed the staircase, looking like the world rested on his shoulders.

"Teagan." He placed a hand on her arm as she too started up the stairs. "Please. I'm worried and my mind is hunting up all sorts of scenarios. Have pity on me."

"Bradbury is our real paw." With that declaration she tugged her arm from within his grasp and slowly walked up the stairs, head down, her slippers dragging on the stairs.

When he could no longer see her, he went into the closest drawing room, poured a hefty amount of brandy into a glass and downed it in one swallow. Refilling it, he took a seat facing the hearth which had burned down to cold embers.

"Their father," he said out loud. "Their father. Damn, what a mess."

The rest of his family came back several hours later and he still sat, drink in hand and facing a cold hearth. He didn't seem to be able to get up and go to his bedchamber no matter how exhausted he was. Or how bad his leg, arm, and ribs throbbed. All he could think about was poor Teagan and what she must be going through.

Finally as the sun began making its way into a new day, he took his weary body up the staircase and down the hall to pause outside her chamber door.

He hadn't made a conscious thought to go there, his body moved on its own accord. Now that he stood outside her door, he knocked, waited, and listened for an answer. When none came, he turned the knob and his pulse accelerated when the door opened and he came face to face with a teary eyed Teagan clothed in her dressing gown.

He opened his arms and without hesitation she stepped into them, wrapping her arms around his waist and resting her head upon his breaking heart.

"I was worried. I should've come sooner." His hands soothingly caressed circles on her back. Her whole body trembled against his.

"Ah'm glad ye'r here with me now. Ah'm sorry ah was rude tae ye last night. Shock at meeting my real paw and hearing the words spoken out loud unsettled me. Ah only wish my maw was here. Ah can tell Bradbury loved her verra much as ah ken she did him as weel."

"I'm sorry for everything and wish I could make things better. But unfortunately I can't bring back the past or the dead. Give Bradbury a chance. Besides Lachlan, he is all the family you have left, unless you want to continue having the duke and Ian part of your family."

"Nay. If ye dinnae mind, ah think ah will go back tae bed. Ah didnae sleep at all last night."

"Rest." He kissed her briefly and left, hoping sleep would make her see things clearly.

LATER THAT MORNING Wentworth sent word that he received a message from Smythe. Sebastian found himself in his brother's study along with Lachlan, Bridgeton, and Myles all anxiously awaiting his brother to share the contents of the letter.

"Some of what I have to say may shock you Lachlan, but please forgive me in advance," Wentworth said as he held the parchment in his hands. Hands that to Sebastian looked to be shaking.

"Smythe made it to Murray Castle and found the duke dead and Ian gone. According to several witnesses, they quarreled and Ian attacked him. When Smythe sent this letter, Ian was nowhere to be found." Wentworth placed the missive on his desk and looked at the faces of everyone in the room. "You are now the Duke of Tremont."

Silence settled around the room. Sebastian waited for Lachlan to say something, anything, but since he didn't speak a word, Sebastian did. "Lachlan, you must go home."

"Ah ken. Ah just dinnae ken what tae feel about what has happened. Ah never wanted Paw...the duke...tae die. Ah just prayed he could become a better mon. Ah need tae go home and make things right. Ah have much atoning tae do on his behalf. And ah need tae see Ian pay for what he did."

"I wish I could travel with you," Wentworth said. "But with Emma expecting I don't want to leave her again, and I must stay for Penelope as well. Sebastian will go with you as I suspect he is not ready to say good-bye to Teagan. Also, and please keep an open mind, Bradbury has requested he accompany you as well. He confided in me he hopes to get to know you and Teagan during the trip. His country estate is in Northumberland, and he will leave you then to see to his lands."

Lachlan's eyes turned to Sebastian and the uncertainty and need he saw in them moved him. Sebastian owed him his life and would do what he could to help him acclimate to being the duke. Sebastian knew firsthand what a task it would be in the coming months. He'd seen Wentworth live through it. Their father had left a mess and Sebastian had a feeling Lachlan's father left an even larger disaster to straighten out. The man didn't sound like he had a heart, and Sebastian wondered how the crofters on Murray lands survived with a tyrant as their duke.

"Should I ask Smythe to accompany you as well?" Wentworth addressed Lachlan directly. "Do you expect any resistance when you arrive at Murray Castle?"

Lachlan paled, then shook his head. "Ah dinnae believe ah need yer mon tae travel with us. My paw was nae a fair mon and a terrible duke. Ah should be a welcome sight. And if ah receive resistance, ah will send word, but ah truly believe the residents in the castle and surrounding lands will breathe a sigh of relief when ah arrive. As for my brother, ah dinnae believe he will set foot on Murray lands. Nae if he wants tae live. And if he disputes the legality of my inheriting, he has nae proof. Just his word against mine. And ah will die and take him with me before ah let him become the duke."

"Good. We have much to prepare because you should leave first thing tomorrow morning. And traveling by coach, my personal coach, will increase your travel time. I was going to suggest a maid travel to assist Teagan, but with Bradbury going as well, the coach will be crowded and I don't believe you want to travel with two as it will only take longer."

Wentworth turned his serious blue eyes on Sebastian, and he swallowed hard. Did he think he would compromise Teagan on the long journey ahead? How did he not know he already hadn't?

When neither he nor Lachlan spoke, his brother continued. "Then it's settled. If you'll excuse me, I have much estate business to catch up on."

Sebastian stayed once everyone else left. He closed the door and turned to his brother. "Thank you for offering me to travel with them so I didn't have to insist."

"You're welcome. She is your future and you belong with her. Just don't be a stranger. And never forget who you are and where you come from."

"Who said I wasn't coming back?"

"My gut. Which is seldom wrong."

CHAPTER SIXTEEN

GOOD-BYES THE NEXT MORNING WERE HARD FOR ALL. Sebastian's sisters didn't want Teagan to leave, and poor Penelope stood to the back looking uncertain. His mother had tears in her eyes and hugged him close.

"Safe travels. Teagan is lovely and I'm happy for you."

"Mother," he whispered in her ear. "Aren't you getting ahead of yourself? I haven't even asked Teagan to marry me."

"You will. I know love when I see it."

"Yes, I do love her and her me, but this may not be the best time for her."

"Nonsense. You marry her quickly, even if your family is not there. We will visit and celebrate another time."

"Thank you." Sebastian swallowed the lump in his throat and fervently hoped he didn't cry in front of his entire family. Two days ago he never would have contemplated living in Scotland, but if that's where Teagan wanted to live, he would as well. They never discussed it, though, so he could be wrong. She could want to live in London for all he knew. Only he doubted she would leave her only brother. At least until he was married and settled. Sebastian had been away from his

family for two years while in America. If he survived that
when he'd left on bad terms, he would survive this. Even
enjoy it. Scotland. Who ever thought?

He hugged each of his sisters, including Penelope and
Emma, and each had tears in their eyes. "I'm not dying. Just
traveling to Scotland. You would think I was moving halfway
around the world."

When Wentworth pulled him in for a quick, hard hug, he
thought he would finally succumb to tears. But he cleared his
throat at the same time as his brother, who looked to be
emotional as well.

"Godspeed," his brother mumbled.

As they made their way down the streets of Mayfair,
Sebastian's eyes were riveted to his surroundings. All was
quiet as they traveled for several miles, and he could feel the
tension inside the coach. Was it because they were leaving
London? Or because Bradbury traveled with them? Or
because of what was awaiting them in Scotland? Mostly likely
all three and more.

TEAGAN'S THROAT hurt and her eyes burned at fighting the
tears trying to escape. She would not cry at leaving her new
found friends. She had to go with Lachlan to Scotland and see
him settled as the Duke of Tremont. She would do her duty
and bury her false father, get to know Bradbury, her real
father, and hopefully come back to London in several months'
time. She loved Scotland and Murray Castle, but her heart
had died the night MacPherson attacked her and the man she
had known as Father tried to kill Lachlan. She would never
stay away from her homeland long, but she wanted to experience London Society and hopefully marry Sebastian and
make a home not too far from his family.

Besides her mother, Lachlan, and her grandfather and uncles, which she seldom saw, she'd never truly had the sense of family. She had found it with the Seabrook's. And she wanted desperately to be part of their family. She loved Sebastian with all her heart, and it seemed only natural they would wed. Her stomach did little flips inside. Perhaps they would not wed? He may have professed his love for her, but he never mentioned marriage. She rubbed her stomach with her hand and closed her eyes to wipe out that thought. Of course they would marry. Why else was Sebastian traveling with them? He looked healed on the outside, but she knew it could take a longtime for broken ribs and an arm to heal. Was he in pain even now traveling in the luxurious coach? She glanced at him across the seat, sitting beside Bradbury. His eyes were cast out the window and his expression, from what she could see, was somber. Did he regret traveling with them? *Stop it,* she chastised. *Ah will nae let my imagination get the better of me. He is here and that is all ah need tae ken.*

After several days of travel, Bradbury broke his silence.

"When I first saw your mother running through a field of lavender, her skirts hiked up to her knees, I nearly fell off my horse. She was that beautiful, and my heart stopped beating as I watched for several minutes. When she finally saw me, she smiled, and something inside me changed forever. I never believed in love at first sight, but that's what it was for both of us."

Teagan could not take her eyes off the man who possessed the title of her real father. He sat up straight and had an air of confidence about him she admired. Even though he looked melancholy. He possessed this compelling charm that made her want to get to know him better.

"I was visiting a university friend at the time, otherwise I never would have met her. Anyway, we met daily in that field for a week. A thunderstorm rolled in one afternoon, and we made our way down the cliff to the beach and into a small cave for shelter your mother knew about." He looked at her and actually blushed. "I will not divulge what happened next, but you both can surmise as you are the result of it. I tried to get out of my betrothal, but my father would not hear of it as the wedding was taking place in a sennight." He paused and exhaled. "I never meant to hurt your mother. We were young and in love and didn't think of the consequences. Two months after my wedding, she sent word about her pregnancy. She panicked, told her father, and he married her to Murray believing him to be a good and fair man. Something he came to regret not long after the wedding vows were spoken. I could not let your mother go. She held my heart. I'm embarrassed to say, I made the long journey once a month so we could meet, but never to..."

Teagan fought tears at the heartbreak she heard in Bradbury's voice. "When my wife and son died in childbirth, I descended into depression and whiskey. I believed their deaths were my fault for betraying my wife. That God was punishing me. A year went by before I pulled myself together and ventured to see your mother again, and when I did, she had given birth to Ian and your father's cruel nature was already in evidence. I begged her to pack you two up and run away with me, but she refused. Said she couldn't leave Ian or the vows she had spoken before God."

Several tears trailed down Bradbury's cheeks, and Teagan knew her cheeks were wet as well. "So I watched from afar until she became too sick to venture out. I am so sorry for all the trouble I have caused. Love is a powerful emotion, and your mother and I could not fight it. I have many regrets, but loving your mother and creating you both is not one of them. I do regret not being the man your mother needed me to be though. I should have stood up to my father and married your mother. But there is no going back. Not now, not ever."

Silence descended on the coach, and Teagan noticed Bradbury looked disheartened and ill. Her heart ached for him, this man who was her father. And she was glad they were having the opportunity to get to know one another. She had a father. A real flesh and blood father who was kind and compassionate and loving.

Next she glanced at Lachlan who looked to be fighting his emotions as well. How could he not after all Bradbury said. Would she perhaps be able to call him Father someday? She hoped so for all their sakes. She needed him and he needed her. Would Lachlan be able to call him Father?

Her eyes ventured Sebastian's way and found he looked as if he wanted to be anywhere but there. She didn't blame him. Not with what had been said.

SEBASTIAN TRIED to close his ears to the extremely personal conversation going on around him, but it was hard when it involved the woman he loved. Watching her emotions play across her face had his heart aching to take her into his arms and comfort her. He might have if Bradbury hadn't been there. But then there would be no reason to comfort her.

Hearing the story of the doomed lovers moved him so he could only imagine how moved Teagan and Lachlan were. He could not wait to have time alone with Teagan so they could talk about it. From his experience woman always wanted to talk about important things, and this was so much more than important. It was life altering.

Sometime later he noticed Teagan had fallen asleep, her head rested on Lachlan's shoulder, and his mind wandered to the rest of the trip. Later that day they would arrive at Bradbury's country estate where they would spend the night. The following morning they planned to visit the blacksmith who helped Teagan and Lachlan, as well as him. Then on to Murray Castle.

With the rocking of the carriage and not having slept well since they took to the road, Sebastian didn't fight the pull of sleep and let it wash over him.

He awoke with a start as the coach came to rough stop and loud voices shouting outside. His eyes locked with Teagan's then Lachlan's as Lachlan pulled a knife from his boot and Teagan did as well. He should have been surprised, but was not. What did shock him was Bradbury did as well. Did everyone carry weapons but him? Bradbury also reached under the seat and removed two pistols. He kept one and handed Lachlan the other. Lachlan then handed Sebastian his knife.

"Do ye ken how tae use a dirk?"

Confused, Sebastian said, "A what?"

"Knife, do ye ken how tae use a knife?"

"Yes." Sebastian took it and tested the feel of it in his hands, hoping he wouldn't have to use it.

"Highwaymen," Bradbury said. "They have been plaguing the area for quite some time."

"We ken. We were hunting them," Lachlan said. "Teagan and ah with the locals for quite some time. Had nay luck."

"They managed to get away from me and my men several times," Bradbury said as he held up the pistol and waited for the door to open. They didn't have to wait long as it was thrown open by a large bearded man who looked more savage than Sebastian thought possible. Was he one of the men who attacked him? Suddenly he had a change of heart about using the knife.

"Do nae move and nobody will get..."

Bradbury put a bullet between the thief's eyes and then all hell broke loose. It would be a long time before Sebastian managed to understand the sequence of events.

A hand reached inside the coach and hauled Bradbury outside. "If ye ken what is good for ye, ye will exit peacefully with yer hands in the air or ah will put a bullet in this English dandy."

"Ian?" Lachlan mouthed to Sebastian, shock on his face.

"We are coming out," Lachlan said as he tucked the pistol inside his waistband and hid it with his greatcoat. Teagan and Sebastian put their knives inside their boots and exited the carriage with their hands in the air.

Five men surrounded them and quickly removed their weapons. "Nice tae see ye again brother...sister. In case ye dinnae ken, Paw is dead. Nae that he was yer real paw." He pushed his pistol hard into Bradbury's temple. "This mon is. What a whore our maw was. Sleeping with a mon before marriage. She deserved what she got marrying my bloody monster of a paw. Unless ye are my paw too?"

"Hell no."

"Too bad. Ah might have let ye live. But now..."

Ian pulled the trigger and Bradbury's head exploded as his body sank into a dead heap. Teagan screamed and ran toward him, only to be held back by Lachlan.

"Dinnae move or ye might be next, sister dear."

Ian proceeded to pace around the three of them while his men held guns aimed at their chests. He paused and looked directly into Sebastian's eyes. A chill crept up his spine at the crazed look in Ian's eyes.

"Tae bad we didnae kill ye weeks ago at the ravine. It would have saved ye from the beating ye got at the cottage and for what ah have planned for ye today. And tae answer the unspoken query, yes. Ah'm the leader of the high-waymen now that Paw is dead. How do ye think he supported us all these years? With Maw's dowry? Stupid fools. We would cross the border and terrorize the English. Which was nae hard, most of them are dandies, asking tae be relieved of their coin and gems. We have amassed quite a fortune. A fortune ye will never get yer hands on Lachlan. Ah wish ye well in running Murray Castle without coin. 'Tis also how ah found ye in the cottage. Ah saw ye both trying tae be brave chasing highwaymen. It was never hard tae shake ye. "

"Ye bloody bastard, ye and MacPherson." Lachlan bellowed. "Ah will hunt ye both down and put ye in the ground myself."

A large, filthy Scot stepped forward with murder in his eyes.

"Easy MacPherson. Right now this is between Lachlan and me." Ian got in Lachlan's face. "Ye think ye will kill me? How? As ah see it, ah'm the one holding the gun. Try anything and the next bullet goes into yer chest. Nae a quick death like Bradbury, but a slow and painful one."

"Why," Teagan said. "Why would ye kill yer own brother?"

Ian moved his black emotionless eyes on Teagan and Sebastian's heart lurched. He had to find a way to keep her safe. Not just from her brother but from her betrothed. Sebastian shivered at the thought of that monster ever having touched her.

"Teagan, my dear sister, ye will be the only one spared. MacPherson still wants ye. Ah cannot fathom why since ye probably whored yerself out to this bloody Englishman just like Maw. As for yer question Teagan, Ah killed paw so ah could become duke. All ah need tae do now is kill Lachlan. After murdering Paw, a brother...is nothing. Besides, ah always hated him."

Out of the corner of Sebastian's eyes, he spotted several men in the woods close by. He recognized the blacksmith. What could he do to let Lachlan and Teagan know without tipping off Ian and his men? He looked at Lachlan and moved his eyes to the woods several times. Finally Lachlan understood and gave him a slight nod. Teagan caught on quickly and nodded as well.

A diversion was what they needed. When Ian's attentions wavered between Teagan and Lachlan, Sebastian lunged at him. He shoved the gun aside, and it went off, taking down the thief to Ian's left. As Sebastian grappled with Ian, out of the corner of his eye he saw men charging out of the woods carrying pistols, swords, and axes. When the other men where dead, including MacPherson, Lachlan helped Sebastian subdue Ian and tie him up. When Ian was secured, he quickly went to Teagan and pulled her into his arms.

"Are you hurt?" he said, praying to God she was not.

"Nay. Are ye?"

Sebastian's legs buckled and took them both down to the ground on their knees. "No. A few bumps and bruises. Ian knows how to fight. But so do I."

"Thank God."

Lachlan took charge. He told George to escort Ian to Bradbury's estate and have word sent to the authorities. With sadness he covered Bradbury's upper body with his cloak. He turned and strode toward Teagan and Sebastian then pulled Teagan into his arms and held her tight against his chest. "Ah thought ah would lose ye."

"Ah as weel."

"We owe George our lives again."

"Aye, we do."

"Ah'm sorry about Bradbury...our father." Lachlan murmured. "He was a good mon. Ian will hang for killing him and for the other crimes committed."

"Aye. He deserves no less. Ah just wish..."

"What lass?"

"Ah wish ah had more time with our real father."

"Me too." Lachlan turned to Sebastian. "Please see tae my

sister. Ah think ah will travel on foot with George tae keep an eye on Ian. Ah will see ye both at Bradbury's Estate."

It was then Sebastian noticed their driver hiding beneath the coach. "Sorry milord, I had no weapon to assist you and a wife and child at home."

"All is well. Let us continue on to Bradbury's Estate."

"Yes milord."

SITTING in the coach with Sebastian's arms around her shaking body, Teagan thanked God they were alive. Only she wished...Sobs rose up from deep inside her soul, and she cried for the man who was her father. The man she would never get to know. Never get to see again. And she wondered if she would ever get the image of his death out of her head? The sound of the gunshot, the spray of blood, and the sound of his body hitting the ground. She hated Ian even more for making her witness it.

When she first realized Ian was leading the band of highwaymen, a sick feeling settled in the pit of her stomach. A stranger would have been easier to deal with. Ian had a score to settle which made him unpredictable. Which he had been. And vengeful. The hateful look in his eyes and on his face had almost paralyzed her in fear for all their lives. They should be thankful Bradbury was the only one killed, but she could not be. She wanted him alive. Wanted a real father, which she never had. Ian stole that from her. But she would have to be satisfied with the time they'd had, and the story he told about her mother and him and the love they shared. Bradbury was gone, and even though she didn't know him long, she mourned him deeply. The only thing that consoled her was both her parents were together at last. She trembled now at the sight of seeing MacPherson and could not feel sorry about his death. He will rot in hell as it should be for his crimes.

"You're quiet. I'm worried about you." Sebastian's soft voice penetrated her thoughts. Thoughts she was glad to leave behind for now.

"Ah'm sad. So verra sad and weary. Ah feel bad for Bradbury and what happened between my maw and him. Did ye hear how he talked about her? He loved her with all his heart and soul. And ah believe she did as weel. He was robbed of kenning us. Ian robbed all three of us from having a relationship."

"I know, love. Fate was unkind to them. Perhaps now they are together."

"That is what ah was thinking just now. That ah prayed they were together at last."

He rubbed the top of her head with his. "I believe they are."

When they arrived at Bradbury's Estate to welcoming servants looking for their marquess, Sebastian gave them the terrible news and asked for a footman to fetch the authorities immediately.

"I beg your pardon, milord," an older gentleman bowed. "I'm the butler, Carson. John, the footman will go immediately with word about the atrocities befallen the marquess. but it may be some time before the authorities reach us here. Hopefully, no more than a day or two. But meanwhile we have dungeons that can house the prisoner."

"Perfect," Sebastian said as Teagan envisioned these dungeons and hoped they were befitting Ian. He deserved the worst for the time he had left on earth.

Not long after Lachlan arrived with Ian they said goodbye to George and the men who helped them. Against her brother's wishes, Teagan followed Lachlan, Sebastian, Carson, and Ian, down a pair of dark, steep stone stairs to the bowels of hell. At least that was what Teagan thought when the stale, musty aroma assaulted her senses. Not to mention the dank chill coming off the stone walls never to dissipate. Yes, she mused. This would be perfect.

Ian had very little to say as he was escorted inside a cell, the bars closed and locked behind him as he slunk down on a filthy cot.

"Please have food sent down twice daily until the constable arrives," Lachlan said as he ascended the stairs. "Ah want him alive and well before he hangs."

Teagan's body shivered at the sound of her brother's voice void of emotion.

Two days they spent in awkwardness at Bradbury's Estate until the constable came to escort Ian to London so he could stand trial for his crimes. Crimes punishable by death. Part of Teagan believed Ian deserved to die for all he'd done. A small part of her did not. Before they left, Bradbury's barrister arrived and told Lachlan that the title and lands that went with it would go to a distant cousin of Bradbury's. However, he had personal revenue and had set up accounts in both his and Teagan's names. They were wealthy.

SEBASTIAN BELIEVED the money would ease Lachlan's burdens at Murray Castle. Teagan appeared not to care about the money. Sebastian felt her slipping away into despair, and he didn't know how to reach her. She seemed distant and quiet ever since they left Bradbury's Estate and traveled, once again, in Wentworth's coach.

He'd never seen Lachlan so withdrawn either and wondered what was going through his mind. Before they left Northumberland, Sebastian had written to Wentworth explaining the situation. He didn't want his brother to hear of Bradbury's death and worry for the rest of their safety.

As they approached Murray Castle, Sebastian took in the well maintained, ancient gray stone castle complete with turrets and what appeared to be a moat that had been filled in, because sure enough, there was a drawbridge. Although it looked to be permanently in the down position. He wondered if it still worked. They went beneath a portico and were greeted warmly by many. Lachlan appeared uncomfortable with the attention, as did Teagan.

After they had time to adjust and mourn the man who had been their real father, Sebastian hoped they would be themselves again. Albeit, only time would tell.

The housekeeper showed Sebastian to his chamber and left him with a promise of a hot bath and food. He paced the chilly room as the fire hadn't been lit. He took care of building it and soon there was a roaring blaze warming his travel weary body. Staring into the flames, he found himself worrying about Teagan. He knew Lachlan would land on his feet. He seemed the resourceful type. Actually, he knew he was. Teagan as well, except it may take longer for her to recover from the shock of witnessing Bradbury's violent death. Sebastian had woken up in a cold sweat several times after reliving the shooting in his sleep. He could only imagine what Teagan was going through.

Perhaps when his bathwater came he could inquire as to the whereabouts of her rooms. He needed to see her. To be reassured she would be fine. His mind and body would not rest until he confirmed it.

After he bathed in the metal tub that barely fit him and had brandy, cheese, and bread, he was reaching for the door when he heard a knock.

"Sebastian, are ye in there?"

Exhaling, he opened the door, took Teagan's hand in his

and tugged her inside the room. After he closed the door, he led her to the fireplace to warm up as her hand was freezing and she was shivering.

"I'm here." He stood behind her, wrapped his arms around her waist and pulled her close, hoping to comfort her and warm her. Whatever she needed, he was there for her.

After a short time she pulled from his arms. "Ah'm feeling better. Ah'm going tae seek out my brother and see how he's fairing."

Sebastian's eyes followed her every move as she walked stiffly toward the door and never looked back. A heaviness settled in the pit of his stomach. He had a terrible feeling she was anything but fine and was slipping away from him.

CHAPTER SEVENTEEN

THE SENNIGHT THAT FOLLOWED PROVED HIS FEARS TO fruition. Teagan took to her chamber and would not leave. Nor would she welcome anyone, including him, inside the walls. The only person allowed in or out was her maid. And when Sebastian stopped her in the hall, her eyes were filled with sadness, and she merely shook her head.

Something had to be done. But what? One morning after a terrible night's sleep, actually—no sleep at all—he knocked on Lachlan's study and entered upon his, "Come in."

"We need to talk." Sebastian sat down without waiting to be invited. He kept forgetting Lachlan possessed the title of duke now. "I'm beside myself with worry about Teagan."

"As am ah," Lachlan said as he rose from his seat and went to the sideboard. He held up a crystal decanter. "Is it tae early, or can we partake in some fine Scot's whiskey?"

"Partake please."

Sebastian took the glass out of Lachlan's hand and downed the contents. "Damn, but that stuff is fine. Burns like hellfire though."

"Wouldnae be good otherwise. Have another, it will go down smooth as silk."

And sure enough it did and took the edge off his nerves. "What do you think is wrong with her?"

"Damn if ah ken. Ah've never seen her like this. Nae even when Maw died. Witnessing Bradbury's gruesome death broke her somehow. 'Tis my only explanation because she is nae a shrinking violet, as ye ken. She rides and shoots better than most mon ah ken. And has never even appeared squeamish when attending tae the injured or sick. Ah think her mind is healing, and the only way she can allow it tae is tae rest in solitude. If it persists much longer, ah will send for the local physician. Although ah will admit, Teagan is a far better healer than he. Dinnae take it personally if she willnae see ye, she willnae see me either.

Another sennight passed and Teagan remained behind closed doors. Sebastian was at the end of his patience and understanding. Why was she ignoring him? Had her feelings for him vanished? Lachlan kept reassuring him, but it didn't help his mind from creating all sorts of scenarios. Scenarios that had him traveling back to London with his heart in tatters. The physician examined her and said she was healthy and eating. She was in shock and could remain that way for some time. He left several bottles of laudanum which Lachlan promptly threw out. Teagan would never forgive him if he gave her any. She always called it the devil drug. She preferred to make her own medicine. Medicine that wouldn't make a person crazy.

Today, a fortnight since he arrived at Murray Castle, Sebastian dressed in his riding clothes, hoping a good long ride would ease his mind. Just as he descended the stone stairs a gentleman, perhaps around forty, leaning heavily on a cane, stepped out of a carriage.

"May I be of assistance?" Sebastian queried.

"Ah hope so. Ah'm looking for Lachlan and Teagan. Ah'm their uncle."

"Uncle. But...I...they...thought you were dead."

"Ah nearly was. Ian is a crazy bastard. Killed Paw and my brother. Left me for dead. Took me this long to recover my wits enough tae even ken who ah was. Came as soon as ah could travel. Had my mon scouring all of Scotland looking for Lachlan and Teagan, only tae find out they were in England until recently. Is that where ye met them?"

"Yes. It's a long story and should be told around a warm fire with a glass of Lachlan's fine whiskey."

"Ah hear he is the duke now? What about Ian? Is he still alive?"

"Let me take you to Lachlan, and he can explain everything that has happened."

Sebastian knocked on Lachlan's study door and entered when the familiar Scottish brogue said, "Come in."

"Uncle Bruce," Lachlan bellowed and stood abruptly, sending his chair crashing to the ground with a loud thud. "Ah thought ye were dead." Lachlan righted the chair then hurried around the desk, pulling his uncle into a hug. "Ah thought tae never see ye again. Is Grandpaw and Uncle Fergus with ye?"

"Sit down, we have much tae discuss."

"I'll just excuse myself." Sebastian backing away toward to door.

"Nonsense." Lachlan waved his arm. "Sit down. Ye ken everything and have been through much with us." He headed to the sideboard and poured three generous glasses of whiskey and handed them out. "Ian told me ye were dead. That he killed ye."

Bruce downed his glass in one swallow and held it out for another. "He bloody hell almost did." He motioned to Lach-

Ian's glass. "Ye might want tae down that before ah begin my tale."

Lachlan tossed the contents of his glass back and looked directly at his uncle. Sebastian, as much as he felt like an intruder, same as when they traveled with Bradbury, knew wild horses couldn't drag him away from what was about to be said.

"Ian came in the dead of night with a ragged bunch of mon. They were nae Murray mon, that is for certain. Or at least ah pray they were nae. He visited Paw's room first and slashed his throat as he slept. Ill-fated on our part that Fergus and ah were visiting at the time, which made it easy for Ian tae kill all three of us in the same night." He took a sip of whiskey. "For some reason ah couldnae sleep that night and was warming myself by the fire when my door was broken down and ah faced Ian and his mon. He told me my sister was dead. As ah processed that terrible news, ah was shot several times. I think each body bastard took a shot at me. The bullet that grazed my head made me forget who ah was for a spell. Hence, why it has taken me so long tae venture out."

He closed his eyes and shook his head. "When ah finally come tae, ah was told Paw and Fergus were both dead, and that Paw's steward sent mon looking for ye and Teagan tae no avail. Until now."

Lachlan topped off his uncle's glass. "The duke wouldnae let us send word about Maw's death. He said he wouldnae have her relatives in his home for her burial."

"Bloody bastard," Bruce growled out.

For the next half hour Lachlan retold the series of events that brought them to this moment in time. Including how they met Bradbury and how he was murdered in cold blood by Ian.

"Ah'm sorry, lad. It shouldnae ever have come tae this."

"Nae yer fault. But we need yer help. Teagan hasnae left

her bedchamber since we arrived here. Sebastian and ah are worried sick over her. As is the rest of the staff."

"Ah'll go tae her now," Bruce said as he stood, leaning heavily on his cane. "Bloody arse, Ian shot me in the thigh and ah will forever need this cane."

"But you live," Sebastian said.

"Aye, ah live. And ah thank the good Lord every day for it."

RESTING IN BED, again for another day, Teagan couldn't seem to get her body to move. Nor her brain to tell it to. She ached in parts of her body she didn't know existed. And her head, it felt three times the size and as though it was used as an anvil by the blacksmith.

She wanted to get up, truly she did. She hated worrying Lachlan and Sebastian. But she just couldn't face anyone yet. Nor did she know how many days she lay here, although she knew the numbers were climbing alarming high.

Last night, in the dead of darkness, she promised herself she would venture outside her bedchamber today. A promise she'd made many times over to no avail. Somehow, when the morning came each day, she couldn't do it. No matter how much she chastised herself for wallowing in self-pity, she could not leave her room. She barely left her bed long enough to take care of her business and change into clean clothing.

So here she lounged in bed once again, a tray across her lap, with her now cold breakfast when a knock sounded at her door.

"Will they never give up?" She huffed believing it to be either Lachlan or Sebastian.

"Go away."

"'Tis yer Uncle Bruce, lass, can ah come in please?"

"Uncle Bruce," she cried as she swung her legs off the bed and stood only to sit back down again as the room spun and her legs gave way. "Come in."

Tears pooled in her eyes when she saw her uncle. He'd aged since she last saw him. Then again it had been several years since her mother took them for a visit. Yet somehow she believed the events of the past months had to do with his aging.

"Teagan, my lass," Uncle Bruce said as he bent down and kissed her cheek. "Ye are a sight for my sore and tired eyes. Ah believed ah would find ye both dead when ah arrived this morning."

Teagan looked at the door, hoping with all her heart her grandfather and uncle Fergus would walk through the door any moment. Her heart weighed heavy inside her chest when they did not.

"What about Grandpaw and Uncle Fergus?"

Resting on the edge of her bed, she listened to the nightmare Uncle Bruce told. Several times, if she hadn't been sitting down, she would have fallen.

"So, what is this ah hear ye refuse to leave yer rooms. Lachlan is beside himself with worry. And ah dinnae have tae tell you, lass, he has had enough tae concern himself with. And a certain Englishmon who cares for ye deeply is even more worried."

"Perhaps today."

"Nay perhaps about it. Ye will leave this room. Ah give ye an hour before ah expect ye in the drawing room."

After her uncle left, all the emotions she'd been suppressing bombarded her, and she lay back on her bed in a heap of sobs that shook her entire body. Feeling...hurt too much. How was she expected to deal with so much loss of life and anger and hatred toward Ian and the man who raised her?

"Ah will nae let Ian win? He willnae ruin my life," Teagan

said as she pulled herself together and rang the bell for her maid.

After a soothing warm bath scented with sprigs of lavender, she dressed in a lovely peach day dress and ventured down the stairs to the family drawing room. Upon entering, she almost turned and ran out. Three sets of eyes stared at her. Her eyes swept over Lachlan's and her uncle's to finally settle on Sebastian's. The blue of his eyes penetrated deep within her soul, and she wondered how she could have been so selfish.

"Lachlan, Sebastian, ah owe ye both an apology. It was never my intentions tae worry ye both. Please forgive me."

Lachlan came forward first and hugged her close. "Nothing tae forgive. Just dinnae do that tae me ever again. Ah was worried for ye."

"Ah ken."

Then Sebastian approached and bowed. "I'm glad to see you up and about."

"Nay need tae be so formal, Sebastian, after all we have been through," Lachlan said.

Sebastian's eyes locked with hers and she nodded her head, suddenly unable to speak. Had he given up on her? Was he just waiting for her to recover her wits to go back home to London? The tremors started in her hands and spread quickly throughout her body. Unable to breathe from uncertainty, she moved forward just as he reached for her and engulfed her in his strong arms.

"Ah'm so sorry ah pushed ye away."

"Nonsense." He pulled back and cradled her face in his hands. The love shining from his eyes melted her bones. "I will never leave you. I love you and with Lachlan and your uncle's permission, I would like to marry you."

"Sebastian," she whispered right before he kissed her.

That kiss conveyed all the unspoken words that were never said between them, and never needed to be said.

He pulled back and smiled. "I take that as a yes."

"Aye, Sebastian Seabrook, ah will marry ye."

Late that night, as Teagan lay in bed, her heart pounded inside her chest as she anticipated Sebastian sneaking into her bedchamber at any moment. She'd trusted her maid with a note inviting him to her room. Too much had happened, and she didn't want to wait until their wedding in a month's time to become intimate. She wanted to become Sebastian's and him hers, in every sense of the word—this very night.

When she heard the creak of the door opening, her hand flew to her stomach and tried to calm the family of butterflies making a home there. It wasn't so much nerves but anticipation for what would come.

"Sebastian," she whispered, suddenly afraid it may be someone else.

"Yes."

She breathed a sigh of relief because for a moment she'd panicked and was thrown back in time.

He strolled to her bedside without saying a word. He didn't need to as his eyes, glowing in the candlelight, expressed all. As he began undressing, her eyes were riveted to his large hands as they unbuttoned his waistcoat. It slid to the ground, soon followed by his shirt, which left him in his breeches and boots. His weight sunk the bed as he sat and removed first one boot then the other. Standing again, he stared deeply into her eyes and goose flesh broke out on her skin and she trembled. His fingers made quick work on the front buttons of his breeches. They slid down his muscular thighs, leaving him naked and powerfully aroused before her.

Her breath caught in her throat at the sight of his manhood thrusting out large and hard from between his thighs. "Is that..."

He grinned a wickedly. "Do not fret, I will prepare you and yes, God created it so it will fit. I believe it will fit you to perfection."

She swallowed. "If ye say so."

"Come," he said with his hand out.

Hesitating for only a second, she crawled to the edge of the bed and stood in front of him on wobbly knees, her arms down by her side and her eyes locked on his face.

"Ah have come."

He chuckled. "Not yet you haven't. But you will."

"Ah will..." Before she could utter another word, he had divested her of her night rail and she stood equally naked and self-conscious while his eyes slid up and down her body from head to toe and back.

"You are beautiful."

Her arms covered her breasts and he gently tugged them aside.

"I will be your husband in a month, no need to be bashful with me."

She went to drop her arms to her side then thought better of it and placed them on his warm, muscular chest instead. Her head tilted up, she licked her lips, and waited for Sebastian to kiss her.

And kiss her he did. He lowered his head and took her mouth with in fierce, savage need. Sebastian devoured her mouth, and then moved on to her neck and lower. All the air escaped her lungs when his hot mouth sucked in her nipple, causing liquid heat to pool between her thighs.

Then he scooped her up into his strong arms, dropped her down on the bed, and covered her body with his.

"What did I ever do to deserve you?" Sebastian murmured as he placed kisses down her stomach while one hand slid up her calf, over her knee to the inside of her thigh —to there.

The moment his hand found her, she arched her back and her body trembled.

"You're ready for me. Had you been thinking about what we had done before while you were waiting for me to come to your bed tonight?"

"Aye."

He positioned his body over hers, nudged her legs open with his knee, and his manhood pushed against her. She didn't want to tense, tried to keep her body relaxed, but it had other ideas at the invasion.

"Relax, my love." Sebastian's mouth covered hers in a kiss that caused the room to twirl. His tongue swirled with hers, he bit her lip with his teeth all the while he pushed more and more inside of her until a piercing pain had her gasping and Sebastian froze.

"I'm sorry."

"Dinnae be. 'tis part of becoming a woman, a lover, and wife."

"Which you will be all of those things to me."

Slowly, he swirled his hips and the pain was replaced with a need to move against him. To feel all that she knew she could now that their bodies were joined.

She met each thrust of his hips with her own and soon they were both gasping as their lungs heaved. Her insides tightened. It started in her stomach and spread below until her insides contracted. She closed her eyes, clenched the sheets with her hands, and let herself fly into the midnight sky.

WHEN SEBASTIAN first entered Teagan's room, he expected her to say she changed her mind and wanted to wait until their wedding night. When she didn't, his insides shook with such a need it took all his self-control to go slow. He undressed first, letting her get a good look at his naked form, hoping to ease her worry. He'd been wrong. It increased her anxiety.

Never in his life had he been with a virgin, so he had to rely on instinct. There would be pain, it was unavoidable. But he would do everything in his power to lessen her discomfort. The truth of it was he would rather cut off his right arm than cause her agony of any kind.

Unfortunately, breaking through her maidenhead could not be avoided. Once he had her on her back and he positioned himself he tried to go slow. He did go slowly until she wrapped her legs around his waist and pushed her hips up into his repeatedly. When her insides clamped down around his cock, he thought he'd died and gone to heaven. The pleasure she brought him spiraled through his body and settled deep inside his heart.

After he collapsed on her, and his breathing returned somewhat back to normal, he rolled off, taking her with him so she was tucked against his side. "I didn't know it could be like this."

She tilted her head up, smiled, and his heart stopped at the love he saw radiating from the depths of her green eyes. "Me neither. But ah thought..."

"Yes. I have been with other women. But let me assure you, never, ever was it like what we just experienced. Being in the arms of someone you love and who loves you in return makes all the difference in the world."

"Good."

He nuzzled her neck. "Good what?"

She sighed and her body curled around his. "Good ye have never experienced such a thing with anyone else but me. Ah want tae be yer everything."

"Haven't you figured it out by now that you are?"

CHAPTER EIGHTEEN

A MONTH LATER AT STONY CROSS MANOR, TEAGAN prepared for her wedding. Since they had decided to make their home in London, they purchased a lovely townhouse not far from the Seabrook family home. Both she and Sebastian had accepted a gracious offer from Emma and Wentworth to hold their wedding at the small chapel on the grounds of their country estate. A chapel she was happy to learn was the place where Emma and Wentworth, Amelia and Bridgton, and Bella and Myles spoke their wedding vows. She could not think of a better place to pledge her love to Sebastian.

Teagan had chosen a lovely pale, yellow silk gown for her wedding dress. Her hair was swept up high on her head with curls cascading over one shoulder. Tiny yellow roses from the manor's rose garden were tucked here and there into her hair making her look like a garden fairie. The butterflies making their home in the rose garden were also present inside her stomach as she anticipated the day to come. Finally, she would marry the man she loved. Become part of his family, which she could naught ever ask for a better family to belong to.

The only sadness she experienced today was tomorrow morning Lachlan and her uncle would travel back to Scotland. She worried overmuch for Lachlan, but Uncle Bruce eased her concerns by stating he would be staying at Murray Castle for an extended period of time. She suspected he didn't relish hurrying back to the Lothian coast since Grandfather and Uncle Fergus were dead. Bruce had never taken a wife. So besides Fergus's wife, their two sons, and several grand-nieces and nephews, he had no family left except for Lachlan and her.

Deep down inside, she was ecstatic Uncle Bruce would be staying with Lachlan. She would still worry overmuch for him, but at least he would not be alone. And perhaps soon he would take a wife. They had already discussed it with him that if by the upcoming London Season, he had not met anyone suitable to become his duchess, he would travel to London. Surely there would be some young debutant to catch his eye. Perhaps even Uncle Bruce might find himself a nice widow and marry. Now that she'd found love, she wanted Lachlan and Bruce to find it as well. Nothing made you more alive and intuitive to your surroundings than love. Colors were more vivid, flowers fragrances more aromatic, birds chirping more melodious. Everything changed for the better.

"Are you ready, my dear," the dowager said as she entered the room and smiled brightly. "You look lovely. I believe my son will lose the ability to speak when his eyes fall upon you."

"Thank ye. And aye, ah'm ready."

"Lachlan is outside ready to escort you to the chapel. Besides Wentworth, Emma and I, everyone else has left."

True to the dowager's word, her brother stood outside her chamber looking pale.

"Is all well with ye?"

"Aye, why do ye ask?"

"Ye look pale."

"Just anxious, happy and sad at the same time," he replied with a crooked grin.

"Has something happened?" Her insides knotted up tight.

"Nay. Well, actually, there is something. Ah hate tae tell ye this on yer wedding day, but ye need tae ken."

"Ken what?" More knots.

"Ian is dead. He died in Newgate in his cell awaiting trial."

"Oh." She moved a hand to her stomach and waited to decipher how she felt about his death. Sad, glad, but mostly sad and angry. The man who raised them made Ian into the monster he had become and for that she was angry. Sad because he never had a chance to be a good man, like his brother Lachlan.

"Half of me wants tae yell with joy and the other half wants tae fall tae my knees and cry for the little boy who dinnae have a prayer in the world of being a good mon, thanks tae that mon."

"Ah ken. Ah feel the same way. But also ah feel guilty for being the elder brother and nae doing something tae help him be a better mon."

"Ye did try, many times ah heard ye trying."

"Aye, ah did.

"Let us nae think of Ian again on this day of my wedding. Ah want today tae be a happy occasion as ah wed the mon ah love."

"Agreed. Now ah'll finish what ah started tae say earlier. Ah could nae have asked for a better husband for ye than Sebastian. But ah'm sad because ah'm going tae miss ye."

"Ah promise tae visit often."

"Ye better. Now let us be off before yer intended thinks ye deserted him."

As Teagan made her way down the narrow, short chapel aisle on her brother's arm, she could not take her eyes off her husband-to-be. Dressed in black formal wear, he stood staring back at her with love shining from his eyes and a smile on his lips. Her insides quivered and her knees weakened. "Look at him," she whispered to Lachlan. "Is he nae the most beautiful mon ye have ever seen?"

Her brother chuckled. "Ah cannot say, lass, as ah never thought of mon as beautiful."

She giggled. "Ye ken what ah mean."

"Ah do. And ah am so happy for ye. Sebastian will never cause ye a moment of worry, nor will he ever be unkind tae ye, and for that, ah am forever indebted tae him. He will spoil ye rotten, as ye deserve tae be."

As they approach the altar, Lachlan kissed both her cheeks and placed her hand in Sebastian's. They faced the vicar united as one.

When he pronounced them man and wife, Teagan could hardly believe it. She'd been in a daze staring into Sebastian's soft blue eyes the entire time and didn't recall speaking her vows. Although she must have, as they were married and walking down the aisle with his family and what there was left of hers congratulating them.

As their wedding feast changed from course to course, Teagan smiled so much her cheeks ached. Once again, the Seabrook family made her comfortable with their informal banter and laughs as they enjoyed the delicious banquet before them. Whenever her new husband looked her way with smoldering eyes, heat pooled down below and she wondered how long they were expected to stay. She didn't have to wait long, as the occupants of the table clinked their wine glasses.

Wentworth stood. "I would like to welcome Teagan into our family. The moment I met you, I knew you were the love of my brother's life and he yours. To Lachlan and Bruce." He turned and looked at each of them. "She will forever be cherished, loved, and safe within our family." He turned back to her. "Welcome into the fold of the Seabrook's." Then he held up his wine glass even higher and bellowed, "To the bride and groom."

Cheers broke out and Sebastian leaned over and kissed her, causing her to blush more than she already had been.

Lachlan stood next and tears pooled in her eyes. "Due tae recent events, ye and Uncle Bruce are the only family ah have left in this world. That is, until ah met the Seabrook family, who have graciously opened their arms tae me as weel. Ah feel blessed. Ah wish ye and Sebastian a world of happiness, many bairns, and a long life."

Cheers broke out around the table again. Before she knew it, she was strolling around the table—her hand in Sebastian's saying their farewells. Bridgeton and Amelie had offered them their estate, which bordered Stony Cross Manor, for their wedding night.

Sitting in the Wentworth's carriage, on Sebastian's lap, had her giving thanks for all the good in her life. A mere three months ago life looked bleak and hopeless. And now, the future beheld more than she could ever imagine all thanks to the man cradling her lovingly in his lap.

"Ah'm thankful we made love already, so ah dinnae have tae be nervous on our wedding night, and ah can enjoy ye having yer wicked way with me."

Sebastian chuckled. "My wicked way with you? Don't you mean you'll have your wicked way with me?"

"That tae," she said as she kissed him, wiggled on his lap, and moaned when his erection pushed against her bottom.

"See." He groaned. "There you go being wicked."

She shifted her body, pulled her skirts up around her waist, and straddled her husband's lap. Her anxious fingers undid his pants, freeing his engorged cock into her waiting hands. She lowered her body, taking him inside her all the way to the hilt, and let out a breathy sigh. "Ah never get tired of having ye inside me. Does that make me a wicked person?

Her husband's laughter caused both their bodies to shake. She ground her hips deep against him and his laughter died, replaced by a loud moan and her lips curled up into a smile right before he crushed her mouth with his and the blissful ride began.

EPILOGUE

"HAVE THEY ARRIVED YET?" TEAGAN SAID TO SEBASTIAN AS she entered the drawing room in early April. She'd been detained due to morning sickness, and she prayed it ended soon as her brother and uncle where arriving today for the London Season. For the next three months their calendar was full with balls, soirées, the opera, musicals, masquerade balls, and more. Her excitement was hard to contain because it was her first Season, even though it didn't really count as she was married. It didn't matter though, she was ecstatic and could hardly wait to introduce Lachlan to the list of eligible young ladies Emma, Bella, Amelia, and she had come up with. And that list included Penelope, who was making her come-out.

"Not yet, my dear." Sebastian escorted her to the settee and kissed her deeply, spreading warmth throughout her body. She may be increasing, but it had done nothing to lessen her desire for her husband. "Sit down. You're positively glowing with excitement. I'm afraid you might fall down."

"Only if ye sit with me and hold me."

He sat, slid one arm around her shoulder, holding her

close, and murmured in her ear, "I love you. Are you feeling any better today than yesterday?"

"Aye."

"Good. I hate seeing you sick, it tears at my heart. I know it's normal in the early stages of pregnancy, but still, I worry."

"Ah love ye. And ah can assure ye 'tis normal and each day ah feel better and better. Can ye believe Bella and ah will deliver in the same month."

"It is exciting, what with Emma and Amelia each having delivered babies recently. An heir for Bridgeton and a spare for Wentworth."

"Can ah confide in ye something?"

"Anything, my dear, anything."

"When ah first met them ah was jealous. The three of them were so happy and in love and married tae wonderful mon. Ah wondered what ah had done wrong in my life tae have experienced such loss, violence, and sadness. And then ah realized ah needed tae encounter all that in order tae meet ye. For us tae meet and fall in love. As tragic as everything was, ah believe it happened for a reason. For us tae be together...forever."

Sebastian turned to her with tears in his eyes. He cupped the back of her head and claimed her lips in a tender kiss that melted her bones. A kiss conveying a multitude of words, the most important one being love.

THE END

ABOUT THE AUTHOR

Christine Donovan is an International Bestselling Author and PAN member of RWA. She is a member of NINC and Rhode Island Romance Writers. She lives on the southeast coast of Massachusetts with her husband and has four grown sons and one granddaughter. When she is not writing or reading, she is either painting or gardening.

Visit her at http://www.christinedonovan.org/ or email her at christinedonovan6@verizon.net